AND THEN There Were Bodies
A Small Town Cozy Murder Mystery

Peyton Stone

Authors Writes, LLC

Contents

Chapter 1

Chapter One

T he interview wasn't going well.

    Still, Luci stuck it out, hoping that maybe it was just a bad first impression. Maybe the guy was nervous and that was why he sounded so infuriating. He might loosen up after a couple of minutes. There was always the possibility he might turn out great.

However, as the interview continued, that probability began to dwindle to about one in a million.

"I'm just pretty much good at everything," the interviewee, Darren Jackson, drawled. He smoothed back his blond hair as if the gesture made him suave as he flashed a cocky and flirtatious smile at Luci. "You name it, I can do it."

They were sitting in Luci's cramped and cluttered office. Dark stained and rough hewn walls encircled the little space, like the sides of a wooden box, sealing the room with no windows. Despite the windowless room, it still had a comforting cozy feel, even if there was only enough room for one desk, two chairs, a couple of filing cabinets, and a tall birdcage in the cramped corner. Lining the walls were several wooden perches that resembled branches along with dangling toys. One of those perches was currently occupied.

"All right," Luci sighed. "Do you know the DDC?"

Darren Jackson's smile faltered. "Huh?" he asked.

That answers that question, Luci thought. Still, she persevered. "The Dewey Decimal Classification?" she prompted.

"Oh. Yeah." The smile was back. "Like the back of my hand."

"All right." She tried not to sound too skeptical. "What's the number for American fiction?" It was 813. Most librarians who had worked any time in the field whatsoever would have known that purely because it was so common.

Darren Jackson paled, evidently surprised to be called out on a lie he hadn't anticipated.

"Um..." he finally said. "Four?"

It took all of her willpower not to sigh in exasperation.

A flutter of wings sounded as a grey blur flew in front of her head to land on the edge of the desk. Simon, Luci's African grey parrot, cocked his head as he regarded the man in front of him then waddled 180 degrees to look at Luci, his yellow eyes surveying her with marked intelligence.

'Not right,' Simon squawked at Luci. Then he tottered back to face the interviewee. *'No further questions. Bye bye.'*

Darren blinked in bemusement, then glanced over at her. This time, instead of a sigh, Luci was fighting back a snort of laughter. Whether he was saying the answer was wrong or he didn't like the employee or—most likely, both, Luci had to agree with him.

"Thank you, Mr. Jackson," she concluded. "That will be all."

Darren laughed as if he thought it was a joke, except when Luci picked up her coffee mug and walked over to the door, holding it open for him, he stared, unmoving.

"You're not hiring me because of a parrot?" he demanded, not moving from his chair.

"No," Luci corrected him. "I'm not hiring you because you aren't what we need right now. Thank you for coming down, though."

Darren opened and closed his mouth in sheer disbelief. Then finally, when Luci remained where she was, door held open in her hand staring back at him, he stood up. He muttered something under his breath about being able to get a better job elsewhere without parrots as he brushed past her.

Luci's office opened onto the break room, so the two walked out in uncomfortable silence until they came to the other door. When Luci stepped through this one, she was right behind the circulation desk of the Mitchell Library.

The Mitchell Library had been built by Luci's grandmother sometime in the '70s, and Luci had inherited it when her grandmother passed away a handful of years ago. It had taken a bit of time adjusting, still though, she loved every inch of the place.

She loved the smell of old books that filled your nostrils as you walked through the narrow aisles. She loved the soft sunlight streaming through the tall arched windows, dust motes dancing lazily in the raking beams. The gentle illumination seemed to make the expansive room glow with warmth, highlighting the honey-hued wood of the endless bookcases. Shadows shifted tranquility over the worn leather chairs as the daylight shifted. The library felt airier and larger than ever under this peaceful glow.

She loved the Bookists, the book club who came in once a month to discuss their latest novel. And, naturally, she loved Simon, who soared overhead as she moved out of the breakroom, flying up to the second story to one of his many roosts. He really was a beautiful bird: slate-grey feathers (except for the red tail feathers), yellow, intelligent eyes in circles of white feathers, and a coal-grey beak. He'd lived at the library since her grandmother had gotten him over a decade ago, and had never been happy anywhere else. It always felt like Simon knew what he was saying. Luci faintly recalled a note left from Grandmother Annabelle tucked into the pocket of Simon's birdcage cover. It had read: *Simon is special, he understands.*

The only thing she didn't love about owning a library was trying to find good employees.

For months now, Luci had barely kept the library afloat through sheer extra hours alone. With only Patrick assisting since her last staffer's dismissal, tasks bordered on insurmountable. The beloved library embodied Juniper's close-knit charm, welcoming loyal locals and tourists alike through its doors daily and she wasn't about to cut down the normal library hours.

Lately though, Luci felt the flames of fatigue licking higher. The passion that first sparked a calling now seemed to be sputtering, desperate for kindling. Before she succumbed to joining the Team-No-Sleep-Overworked-Business-Owner club, she had begun the arduous journey of finding a new hire. So far, none of them had met her standard.

Luci watched Darren Jackson stalk out of the building. Patrick, who was standing behind the circulation desk, putting books on the trolley to reshelve them, watched along with her.

"No go, I take it?" he asked, brushing the mop of light brown hair out of his face.

"No go," confirmed Luci, more than a little bitterly. She had really hoped this one would be a winner. His résumé had looked good, but clearly, he'd been lying on it. Even if he hadn't been, she wasn't sure if she would have been able to stand his personality for more than a few minutes.

"Shame," Patrick tsked. "Would be nice to have someone else to help carry the load."

Luci shot him a side-eyed *really*? look.

"I'm just saying..." he held up his hands in conciliation.

"Trust me, I know." She glanced down at the pile of letters on the circulation desk and sighed. It had been months since she let Alva, the former staffer, go. Luci had discovered Alva was conspiring with a well-known land mogul to devalue the Mitchell Library in an attempt to force her to sell.

Even though they really needed that extra person, it seemed as though said person was never going to show up. There was too much to do. Patrick was reshelving the books, while she had to check finances, look at inventory, catalog the new books, find time to clean, help guests—

She forced herself to mentally stop before she spiraled too far. She couldn't afford to spiral. There wasn't enough time.

Glancing down, Luci noticed she was carrying around an empty coffee mug. It really shouldn't have been a surprise, given her addiction. True as that may be, she hadn't realized how quickly she had downed the last cup. She hurried back to the breakroom, refilled her mug from the hall-filled carafe, and, almost as an afterthought, grabbed one of the white chocolate cranberry scones she had baked yesterday and brought in. By the time she reemerged, Patrick had vanished into the aisles with the grey trolley.

Munching on the scone, and careful to make sure all—okay, most—of the crumbs landed on the napkin, she began opening the mail at the circulation desk.

Most of it was junk mail. One was a physical copy of a résumé, which she didn't even realize people did anymore, considering she posted the job opening online. Another was a letter from a colleague in Denver about a library sale, asking if she wanted to take any of the books before opening the sale to the public. Another was a standard, bubble-lined manila envelope with no return address and a lump sealed inside.

Luci froze momentarily, her mind instantly going back to a few months ago when she'd received a similar letter that had set off a chain of events leading to her sister's arrest and subsequent release when Kris was found innocent. Part of her wondered if the same type of thing was about to happen.

Sensing her dread, Simon's rough, but clipped talons settled onto her shoulder as he landed - that familiar presence she'd felt a thousand times. He leaned closer to her face to nuzzle it affectionately.

'Bad?' Simon asked.

"No, Luci replied. "Just a letter."

I'm being paranoid, she thought to herself. Without hesitating further, she tore open the envelope, her curiosity overpowering any second thoughts.

The lump, it turned out, was a small coffin-like wooden box, no longer than the palm of her hand. She gently shook it, a rattling noise letting her know something was inside. She unlatched the tiny brass clasp and the box's secret tumbled out, hitting the counter with a musical chime. A key glittered in the morning light before her. As Luci lifted the brass key to examine it closer, she was surprised by the weighty metal as she pondered the antique's origins.

Pondering what this key might open, Luci flicked her eyes back to the box, where an intricately folded piece of paper framed the coffin-shaped box. Gently setting the key on the counter, Luci extracted the single piece of paper. With an eyebrow raised curiously, Luci unraveled the tri-folded piece of paper to slowly reveal a short message:

This should have been your grandmother's. I'm sorry it's taken me so long to give it to you. It's time to right a grievous wrong. I only wish I'd had the courage to do it sooner.

Luci tilted her head, rereading the message, almost as if she anticipated a more detailed explanation to materialize. Despite her best efforts to decipher any further meaning, it stayed stubbornly vague. No hidden message revealed itself no matter how much she tried to interpret more from what was already written. Those four cryptic sentences only left her with more questions than answers.

My grandmother? Luci wondered. Her grandmother, Annabelle, had been dead for over five years now, having passed in her late '70s. Why would anyone be telling her that this key should've been her Grandmother's? Why wait? And it was clear that whoever had sent the message knew Grandma Annabelle was dead. Why bother sending it to Luci?

"Right a grievous wrong?" she muttered, bewildered. She glanced at the key. The key was old, thicker than modern keys, and heavy. While not excessively aged, it bore the gentle hallmarks of time passed. Running her thumb along the cool metal, as she glanced back at the note, answers to her growing list of questions still eluded her.

Something told Luci she didn't want to know what the key opened.

Chapter 2

Chapter Two

It happened as she was pulling out a tray of chocolate chip cookies. She was so excited by the revelation that she nearly dropped the tray. She'd been baking at home alone, fixing herself a consolation treat for almost getting a new hire and musing over the key when it finally hit her what the key was for. It should have been obvious, really. The moment Luci thought about it, she knew she was right.

In the basement of the library was an old locked door. It had never been opened in the entire time Luci had acquired the library.

When Luci was a child, she asked her grandmother what was in the room. "It's your grandfather's room," her grandmother had explained several times. Whenever she said this, Luci would immediately follow up with, "Why don't you open it?" Her grandfather had died in the '80s, and her grandmother had always seemed so sad when she talked about him that Luci hadn't prodded much. Whether or not her grandmother had ever opened it, Luci didn't know. If she had, Luci wasn't around to witness it. Once Luci had inherited the library, she looked for the key that might open it, but it was nowhere to be found. She kept intending to call a locksmith to open the mysterious door or simply have a contractor come and break it down. However,

Luci never got around to it; too many other priorities filled her days. With scarcely a stray thought of the abandoned basement room over the past several years, the dusty secrets that lay behind that door had now catapulted to the forefront of her mind.

Now, as she bit into a cookie still so warm that it was falling apart in her hand (the best way to eat chocolate chip cookies), she tried to remember what the door looked like as her heart began to race excitedly. She couldn't be 100% certain since she had barely looked in the door's direction in months, as it was tucked away in a far corner of the basement, but if her memory was correct the knob was brass- the same color as the key she'd been given. Considering the door hadn't been touched in nearly forty years, it had an old lock, which would fit her guess on the key's age.

Who else would have that key if not her grandmother? Why would someone have held onto it for all these years? Most importantly, why would someone choose now to send it back, *after* her grandmother's death?

The more she thought about the key, the more questions were raised. She was almost certain that she had solved the first question of what the key unlocked. Mid-bite into the soft chocolate-chip cookie, Luci felt its comforts outweigh her curiosity about the chilled basement shadows. The cookie's velvety sweetness warmed her belly, far outweighing the locked door's mystery's hook for now. She didn't mind waiting until the next day, to see if her prediction was correct.

***

Luci arrived at the library early in the morning. It was chilly, the mid-October air just beginning to show signs of cooling down for winter. In the distance, the Juniper ski slopes at the edge of town were still green and would remain so until early November when the addition of fake snow would herald the start of the ski season. Until then, they were just bare strips through the trees, like a finger drawn through flour. Still, just looking at them and feeling the change in the air was enough to make her itch to get back out onto the slopes.

Luci had lived in Juniper, Colorado all her life except for a few years away before returning to help with the library. In the almost thirty years since she was born, she witnessed the transformation of the quiet, not-even-on-the-map small town morph into a bustling tourist spot in winter. In summer, hikers would explore the miles of mountain trails before winter's snowy blanket put them to rest for the winter. Though expanded infrastructure now catered to tourism, the town had somehow preserved its signature charm—even as crowds sometimes felt larger than the town could handle.

When she entered the library, the chill had permeated the building, but not enough to convince her it was time to start running the heat. She started her normal routine: release Simon, brew coffee, ingest a minimum of two cups of said coffee while she set up for the day and answer emails. Then she would walk around the library with Simon to make sure everything was in its place before opening at nine.

Today, however, about an hour before opening, she fished the mysterious key out of the top drawer in her desk and walked down to the basement. As she approached, a familiar weight landed on her shoulder.

'Why basement' Simon squawked, tilting his head and looking at her curiously. *'No bad.'*

"No, nothing bad this time." Luci reached up and stroked his feathers. "Because I want to see if a theory of mine is correct," she answered.

Simon flicked a wing irritably as if he didn't believe her. She couldn't blame him. Most of the time, when she had to go to the basement, it typically meant annoying repairs. Despite being a parrot, Simon knew the library well enough to know that there wasn't anything 'bad' with the library this morning.

"You don't have to come with me, you know," she reminded him.

Simon flicked his wing out again, this time deliberately swatting Luci's cheek as if offended by the statement.

"Suit yourself," she warned as she twisted the knob and opened the door to the basement.

Old wooden stairs leading downward into darkness greeted her as she pulled open the door. Her fingers wrapped around the familiar string that would turn on the light and tugged.

The single lightbulb illuminated the rest of the stairs, covered in grime. A cobweb ran from the ancient wooden railing to the cement wall the flimsy rail was attached to. The unpleasant scent of musk that seemed to always come with old basements, no matter how hard you tried, hit her nose as she descended.

When she reached the floor, she fumbled around until she found the string for the next lightbulb. Three lights shone this time, letting her see the entirety of the basement.

Large concrete blocks lined the whole room, the foundation was cracked in some spots and covered in grime. On the wall closest to the stairs were the water heater and the circuit breaker for the building, the only reasons she ever came down here.

It wasn't large, making up only a fraction of the square footage above. It had always struck Luci as a bit odd how small the basement had seemed, but she hadn't given it much thought until now, as she held the old, heavy key in her hand. She had to wonder if the answer was behind the locked door. She had no idea how large the area behind the door might be; for all she knew, it could span the entire rest of the building.

The door still looked incredibly sturdy. The paint was chipped and peeling in some spots, and she could tell even in the dim light that the handle was covered in grime. There was no doubt the door would stand for another hundred years if left on its own. It felt like the epitome of 'they don't make them like they used to.'

The key fit perfectly into the hole. She was surprised at how fast her pulse was beating and how her heart felt like it was about to burst from her rib cage in excitement.

She twisted the key. There was an unpleasant scraping sound as pins that hadn't moved in years were forced from their resting spot. Finally, there was a click, and the door swung open.

It was dark inside. The lights from behind her only illuminated the area immediately before her, leaving the rest of the space in utter blackness. Something about the unknown void in front of her sent a chill running along her arms.

Or maybe that was just from the cold of the basement.

"You'd tell me if you'd been down here before, right, Simon?" she asked. Though Simon was a parrot, talking with him proved strangely comforting, more so than many humans she knew. His steady gaze would fix upon her with patient understanding as she gave voice to brewing feelings. Occasionally he mirrored portions back in a parroted fashion.

'New place,' Simon responded. He shifted on her shoulder as if considering taking off, but he stayed where he was.

"Right," she muttered and pulled out her phone. A moment later, her flashlight flicked on. It took her a moment, but she eventually found another string and yanked it down, illuminating the area in yellow light.

It was a cluttered room that wouldn't have been out of place in an antique shop. Several metal shelves had been lined up in rows and were laden with old relics, none of them dating past 1980, if she had to guess. Maybe earlier. Old suitcases, kid's toys, cardboard boxes without labels that were sagging at the bottom as if about to split open at any moment, an old radio. And that was only the first aisle.

In one corner was a long wooden table with papers and tools strewn about. It looked like some sort of craft or work table. She could see a hammer and chisel among the items. An old lamp covered in cobwebs sat on it, and a dirty, rusting pickaxe rested on the wall nearby. A dusty wooden stool sat in front of the workstation, the legs looked like they were rotting through.

She decided to circle the perimeter first before examining the desk. Everything was covered in so much grime and dust that just looking at it was enough to make Luci want to sneeze. It was also freezing, even more so than the rest of the basement.

Then Simon launched himself from her shoulder, stirring up the nearby dust causing her to sneeze. Several times. Her eyes watered as her nose began to run. She hated dust with a passion.

'Luci come.' Simon's voice sounded from the far end. *'New thing.'*

"It's all new things," Luci retorted. "Well, actually, they're all old things that are new to me since I've never seen any of this stuff before."

There were so many fascinating trinkets and objects in the room. It seemed a shame that it had all been locked up until now. Why, though?

'Luci come.'

Rolling her eyes at Simon's persistence and wiping her nose, she followed the parrot's voice, moving past more rows of curios and antiques she had never realized were down here.

It sounded as though Simon was fluttering around the last row. When she rounded the corner, however, she stopped dead in her tracks. Her lips parted, eyes widening in shock. Her phone clattered to the ground, her fingers numb, as she stared at what was in front of her.

It was a skeleton lying on the ground, limbs splayed at unnatural angles. Its face was staring at Luci, and surrounding the skull like a halo was a large dark stain on the floor. A stain that was unmistakably dried blood.

A chill raced up her body as she stared at the skeleton, trying to make herself believe what she was seeing. It seemed impossible, but no matter how many times she blinked or how often she looked away and back, it was still there.

Now she knew why the room had been locked all these years.

Chapter 3

Chapter Three

"There's a skeleton in my library," Luci said nonchalantly into the phone.

"What?" the person on the other side of the line asked, the masculine voice filled with bewilderment.

"It's Luci, by the way."

"Yeah, if the name on my caller ID hadn't told me that, the fact that you're the only library owner in my jurisdiction would have clued me in," replied Detective Daniel Flinn. "Please tell me you're talking about a plastic skeleton you're using as some Halloween decorations and not an actual skeleton."

"Real," Luci stated. She paused. "At least, I'm pretty sure it is. It's not like I'm an expert in these things."

There was a scuffling on the other end of the line, as Daniel was grabbing things before heading to the car. "In that case, please tell me that you aren't using a real skeleton as Halloween decorations."

"I'm not *that* into Halloween," Luci assured him.

"Right. I'll be there in a few minutes."

About ten minutes after she called, a familiar figure appeared on the other side of the glass front doors. Luci hurried over, unlocking the door before he even had the chance to knock.

"Hey," Luci greeted.

"Hey yourself." Daniel flashed her a small grin. He was tall, with striking red hair and green eyes. "How have you been?"

"Until now? I've been all right," Luci managed a weak smile, sighing. "How about you?"

Luci had seen little of Detective Daniel Flinn since her Bookists club friends Nick and Petra's engagement celebration. She recalled Daniel's inadvertent involvement - he had covertly gathered club members to arrange Nick's library proposal that day. Fortunately, Petra said yes.

In the months since Daniel barely visited - just once or twice for casual check-ins as he had known Luci since she reported finding a body last summer. Be that as it may, no substantial interaction had passed between them until today's unexpected discovery.

"Been all right," he shrugged, stuffing his hands in his pockets as he looked around. "Nothing particularly eventful since, well, you know." He shrugged. The fluorescent lights glinting off his head made his orange hair look like it was alive. "It sounds like that might have changed, though."

"Yup, slightly."

Daniel opened his mouth, presumably to ask her to show him where the skeleton was, but before he could do that, a rustle of feathers and an excited caw signaled Simon's arrival, moments before he descended onto Daniel's head.

'Daniel here,' Simon announced, tilting his head to look down at his living perch. His red tail feathers twitched. *'Luci Daniel.'*

"Yes, I know he's here," Luci acknowledged. "I'm the one that called him."

'Hi hello.'

Daniel grinned, eyes practically rolling back in his head as he looked upward at the parrot. "Hey there, Simon," he expressed cheerfully. "Good to see you, bud."

'There's a skeleton in the library,' Simon informed Daniel sagely.

"He knows," Luci expressed. "Why else would he be here?"

Simon paused, cocking his head as if considering the question.

'See Simon' he suggested.

"It can be both," Daniel suggested. He reached a finger up to his hairline. Simon regarded it for a moment. After he deemed it a worthy perch, he stepped onto it, and Daniel brought Simon down to eye level. Daniel ran a knuckle along Simon's chest. "He is the library Overlord, after all."

"Not you too," Luci groaned. "It's bad enough that Nick has practically bowed down to him."

'I am Overlord,' Simon squawked proudly.

"Just please tell me you didn't bring him human food?" she made a wry face.

"Not this time," Daniel chuckled. He moved his finger over toward his shoulder, prompting Simon to hop over to his new roosting spot. "Granted, when you said 'skeleton in the library' I kind of dropped everything and headed over. No time for food."

"Thanks for coming so quickly," Luci responded. "I mean, it's probably nothing. It's more than likely an old prop or something. A very *realistic* old prop."

"Did your grandparents make props?" Daniel asked, arching an eyebrow.

"Nope," Luci replied, with a shake of her head. "Now that I think on it though, locked room and all, it's the only rational theory I got other than someone got whacked in the basement without my knowing."

"Well, then," Daniel surmised. "I suppose we should get down to the basement and see if your grandparents started a side prop business that never came to fruition.

Luci hurriedly put up a note saying they would be opening late. Patrick was supposed to start his shift at nine, but considering he seemed allergic to punctuality, that typically meant he would get there around 9:30. In short, they wouldn't be disturbed for a while.

Luci and Daniel walked in silence across the library as Simon soared overhead. She hadn't closed the basement door or turned off any of the lights, so the basement was fully visible as they descended.

"It's in there," Luci directed, pointing to the gaping door. The key still jutted from the lock.

Daniel nodded. He must have seen the uneasy expression on Luci's face because he paused and asked, "Do you want me to go in front?"

"No, no," she insisted, steeling herself. "Let's get this over with."

She led him into the room and through the aisles. It was like walking through a time capsule of the seventies, though with substantially more dust.

When they rounded the corner, Daniel froze. He regarded the body from a distance, his eyes seeming to scour every inch of it before his eyes began darting around the immediate area. It was like he was trying to take in everything at once. Luci felt a little uneasy to see him in full-on detective mode, unsmiling and serious, his posture rigid.

After he had taken stock of everything from a distance, he stepped closer to bend down and silently examine the bone. Sucking air between his teeth, he stood, a frown forming on his handsome face.

"Well, it's definitely real," he concluded. "And he was most certainly murdered."

"How do you know?" she asked. "I mean, there's the stain on the floor, which I'm assuming is probably blood. Perhaps that was there before, or maybe he fell and hit his head."

He raised an eyebrow. "There's a bullet wound in his skull."

"What?" She raced over to stand next to Daniel. She couldn't believe it. She had assumed she had been overreacting, or at least, had been hoping that she was overreacting. Even as her eyes betrayed the truth before her, Luci still couldn't believe there was an actual skeleton in her basement. Her Grandparents weren't into props after all.

Her gaze followed where Daniel had crouched down again pointing. Her eyes focused on the front of the skull. And there it was. A hole right on the forehead with cracks radiating from the jagged and sharp edges.

"I don't know much about forensic anthropology," Daniel confessed, crouching down to look closer. "Even so, I'm fairly certain that's a perimortem GSW."

"Perimortem?" Luci wracked her brain. "Around death?"

"Working in a library pays off again," Daniel noted, looking over at her with something that might have been an impressed look.

"More like barely passing two years of Latin," Luci responded. "But I have no idea how to identify something like that."

"I only know a bit myself." Daniel scooted toward the skull to study the wound more closely. "Perimortem trauma are injuries that happen around the time of death. Antemortem trauma, injuries that happened before death, would show some signs of healing. There would be evidence of bone repairing and stuff like that. Don't ask me how to tell the difference between postmortem and perimortem, though. I never understood that part."

"Hence detective and not forensic scientist?" Luci quipped. Daniel turned to glance at her, the edge of his lip curling upward.

"I was never very good with the sciency part," he admitted. "Here, I can see there isn't any sign of healing. Not only that, I can't imagine anyone would shoot a skeleton just for kicks. The stain is undoubtedly blood."

He stood and stretched and then took a second look at the skeleton, the corners of his lips pulling downward. "I mean, this is all speculation," he added. "I'm not an expert. I only came by myself to make sure it was worth calling in. I'm going to call the station and get the cavalry over here. They'll be able to get the answers we need to find out what really happened here."

"So what you're saying is... the library's closed today," she surmised.

"Unless you want to explain to your patrons why there are a bunch of crime scene investigators roaming around your basement, probably," Daniel shrugged. "Although that brings me to another question."

"And what's that?"

He turned to face her. "Why are you only finding this body now?" he asked. "I don't think you're the type of person that will literally hide a skeleton in their closet, and this one has been here for I don't know how long. Why didn't you report it years ago?"

"Because I didn't have the key until yesterday." Luci explained the whole story: the letter, finding the key, and why she hadn't felt the need to open the door before. Daniel listened quietly, nodding.

When she finished the admittedly short story, he noted, "I'll need to see the note. And probably take the key."

"Yeah, of course."

They walked back upstairs, Simon soaring above them, clearly irked that she had closed the door behind her to prevent him from flying down there again. They walked back into her office and Luci rummaged around until she found the paper.

"Thanks," Daniel muttered, as she showed him the letter. He scanned it, his lips mouthing the words as he did. Then he looked up, studying her with interest. "Have you noticed trouble seems to have a way of finding you?"

He said it light-heartedly, a smirk playing on his lips. On the other hand, something about the words made her skin prickle uncomfortably. She tried to laugh it off.

"Maybe the library is cursed," she joked, her voice a little hollow. "It is Spooky Season, after all."

'Cursed Spooky Season,' Simon squawked cheerfully, flying down to rest on the circulation desk between Daniel and Luci.

The words sounded a little too ominous for Luci's liking.

Daniel was reading the words over again with interest. It seemed impossible that he was gleaning that much out of the short, four-sentence message, regardless, he was scrutinizing it as if it would hold all the answers, instead of just raising more questions.

As she thought about the letter, four words floated to the front of her mind that sent a new chill through her.

Right a grievous wrong.

And what was more grievous a wrong than an unsolved murder?

Chapter 4

Chapter Four

L uci stared at the computer screen on her desk, trying to force herself to focus on figuring out what books were in high enough demand that she should grab more copies and which of their current stock was in such disrepair that they needed to replace them. The words blurred together on the screen, seeming to become an infuriating jumbled mess that she couldn't decipher.

She sighed and pushed away from the desk, moving her stare from the computer screen to the ceiling.

It was the room downstairs. She couldn't get it out of her head. Forensics had been in and out all day, collecting the skeleton and any other evidence they'd found along with them. She'd tried to ask Daniel what they'd found, but he hadn't told her much, only that he would keep her posted when he could.

She had tried to shove the room from her mind. But of course, she couldn't. It had been her grandfather's room. There had been a body in a locked room in her library that her grandmother had told her to leave alone. Had her grandmother known? And what about her grandfather? It had been his room, after all. And that meant...

She didn't know much about her grandfather. He'd died before she was born, and her mother hadn't told her much about him, either. What little she had heard was that he had been a good man with a great sense of humor who loved his wife, Annabelle, more than anything else in the world. That didn't seem like the kind of person who would hide a body in a hidden room in their library.

Running her fingers through her hair, she sighed, grumbling to herself. She didn't have time for this. She had too much on her plate already. She didn't need to add 'mysterious skeleton who had been locked away in the basement for nearly forty years' to her list of things to worry about.

She sat back up and turned toward her computer, clicking over to a browser with several tabs open, all correlating to a different applicant's résumé. She needed to work. If she couldn't focus on inventory, she might as well try and solve another of her major problems: finding a new employee.

There were a couple of promising applicants. A woman named Lauren had been working in libraries for over twenty years and had a master's in Library Sciences. Another applicant named Raymond was around her age and seemed to have as much experience as Luci herself had. The last candidate, James, looked like a risky gambit but might be worth interviewing in person.

She wondered how any of them would react to hearing about her finding a skeleton in the basement.

She sighed. She'd lasted a grand total of ten minutes before thinking about it again. She wasn't going to be able to leave it alone. A skeleton had been in her library for decades and she'd never known. She needed answers and there was only one place she might find them.

She stood and headed out of the office.

Patrick was behind the counter, talking to a regular about which fantasy book she should check out next. He glanced over at Luci when she appeared.

"Hey, Luci," he called. "Sarah likes dragons, magic, and politics and has already read all the *Game of Thrones* books. Any recommendations?"

She barely had to think about it. "*Priory of the Orange Tree*," she shared. "Covers all the bases. A bit different than GoT, but a great read. Though fair warning, it's a massive book."

Sarah nodded her appreciation and hurried over to the fantasy section of the library.

"You all right?" Patrick asked. "You look a little off."

"I'm fine," Luci breathed heavily, running her fingers through her hair. "Just a lot to deal with, all things considered."

Patrick snorted and nodded. "Skeletons in basements will do that to you. You really should have closed for another day."

She eyed him. "Are you saying that because you care about my well-being, or because you really wanted to have another day off?"

He shrugged. "Why can't it be both?" he asked.

Luci shook her head in fond exasperation. For all his laziness, she liked Patrick. She always thought he looked a little out of place at the library. With his flannel button-downs and denim jeans, he looked more like he should be out chopping wood. She knew why he liked working there, though. A large stack of books sat next to him on the counter, and she had a funny feeling that none of those were books destined for the return cart.

"Are you really planning on checking out all of those books at once?" she asked.

"Um...yes?" he grinned. "I would keep them here and read on the job, but last time I did that, you told me to knock it off."

"Of course I did," Luci chuckled. "Because you were hiding away in the breakroom reading a pulp sci-fi thriller instead of helping people find books of their own."

"That wasn't my fault," Patrick protested.

"Oh really? Then whose was it?"

"The author's," he stated, with such sincerity that Luci nearly believed him. "He's the one that put the compelling plot twist right when my break was supposed to be ending."

Luci smirked despite herself. She couldn't really be mad at him, not when she'd done the same thing at least a handful of times over the years.

"Just make sure you don't forget these for six months like you did last time," she joked. "I can't have you going off with half the library and not returning it."

Patrick gave a sheepish smile but she noticed he didn't promise her anything. Not that she expected him to.

"I've got to check something," she told him. "I'll be back in a bit. And no reading at the circulation desk." She added the last bit when she saw him reaching for the top book in his little stack. He retracted his hand immediately and started whistling innocuously.

At least my remaining employee likes books, Luci thought as she strolled through the library. *Now I just need to find one who also likes to work and isn't chronically late.*

She walked down the basement steps, turning on the lights as she did. The stairs creaked under her weight but held her as always.

The door to the mysterious room was closed again but unlocked. She'd been given the all-clear yesterday evening, so there was nothing to stop her from looking. Daniel had taken the key yesterday, along with the strange note, to test for prints even though he hadn't sounded particularly optimistic about the likelihood of finding anything. It was clear that whoever sent the note didn't want to be found. Besides, any prints on the key would have been obscured by Luci's own when she'd handled it. Still, it was worth a shot.

She wasn't sure what to expect when she walked inside, how different it would look, or what they might have taken, so she was a bit surprised that it was the same as it had been yesterday. The only difference was the lack of a skeleton.

This time, she wandered the other aisles that she hadn't gone down, trying to see if there were any clues that might tell her what had happened. She crouched down to look at the suitcases. The letters JM were embroidered on one set, and AM on the others. Joseph and Annabelle Mitchell. No surprise there.

As she explored the room more thoroughly, she couldn't help but notice a few strange things. The first was that a lot of the items in the room, though now at least 40 years old, looked as though they might have been brand new or close to it when they were put in here while some of the items looked as though they had barely been touched. There were items that were valuable and others that would have been back in the day. These items had been left in here to gather dust, as if the room had been locked up in a hurry.

The second thing she noticed that piqued her interest was the room itself. The walls were made of different materials than the rest of the basement, and the library in general.

She ran her fingers along the rough stone in contemplation. They came back covered in grime.

If she didn't know any better, she would have said that this room was built at a different time than the rest of the library. She'd thought the entire building had been constructed in one go in the '70s, yet if that were the case, then wouldn't this room look more or less the same as the rest of the basement?

A draft brushed across her skin and she shivered. It was always cold down in the basement, and the threat of looming winter made it even worse.

She finished circling the mysterious room, ending at the work table. The papers strewn there were old and barely legible, but they were large, the type of paper used for schematics for something. The well worn tools consisted of a few old screwdrivers, a hand saw, a chisel and a few others. Her grandfather had gotten his fair use out of them, it would seem.

Below the work table was an old metal toolbox that she hadn't noticed earlier. The edges were rusting, but it still looked as though it was in good condition. The metal was cold against her fingers as she pulled it out from its resting spot.

The case was gray, and rustier than it had looked beneath the table, but still held together. The smell of old metal hit her nose and seemed to fill her mouth.

She reached out to open it, then paused. She was up to date on her tetanus shot, but that didn't mean that playing around with a rusty box without gloves was a good idea.

Common sense won out over curiosity, and she ran back upstairs. She kept a pair of heavy duty gloves in her office because of all the repairs she'd had to do a few months ago. As she hurried to the office, she noticed Patrick out of the corner of her eye, slamming a book shut and pretending he hadn't just been reading. She didn't bother lecturing him. She had more important things to do.

The gloves were in one of the less cluttered drawers in her desk. She grabbed them and began shoving her hands impatiently into them as she hurried back to the basement.

'Go to basement', Simon asked as he landed on her shoulder.

"Yep. You stay up here for right now."

Simon glared at her with one yellow eye, clearly offended by the request.

'My library,' he claimed, and before she could argue with the surprisingly stubborn parrot, he launched himself from her shoulder and swooped down ahead of her.

"It's not your library," she grumbled as she followed the bird. Simon retorted with a caw that sounded a little too much like a dismissive laugh for Luci's liking.

Simon was flying through the room when she got there.

"Just, be careful where you land," Luci insisted.

Simon fluttered onto the worktable and waited for Luci to arrive. She stroked the bird through the thick gloves before crouching in front of the box.

When she opened the toolbox, she wasn't surprised to see several tools piled together inside. What did surprise her were the types of tools she found inside. She pulled them out one by one, and the more she extracted, the more confused she became.

Hammer, chisel, screwdrivers… all tools that were identical to the ones on the worktable. She knew it wasn't necessarily unusual for workers to have different sizes of tools for different jobs. However, these were the same size and shape as the ones she'd already noted. It wasn't necessarily out of the question that he would want two sets of tools if they were located in two different places. Still, something about the setup made it seem odd.

She dusted off her gloves as she examined the contents a second time. She was probably just being paranoid. People had duplicate tools all the time.

'What's wrong' Simon asked, tilting his head to study her.

"Nothing," Luci muttered. "Everything's fine."

She shuddered inwardly. She wasn't so sure she believed herself.

Chapter 5

Chapter Five

The door to the house opened, and Luci heard the tell-tale sound of Kris throwing her keys onto the table by the door.

"Hey there," Kris drawled, hopping into the room and throwing her jacket onto the couch. She kicked off her flats, which went sliding across the floor until they hit a wall. Her chestnut hair, the same color as Luci's, was pulled back into a bun until Kris undid it and let it fall down her back. It was Kris' regular 'get out of work mode as quick as possible' routine.

"Hey yourself," Luci responded, putting her book down and stretching. "Scones in the kitchen, by the way."

"Thank god," Kris called over her shoulder as she hurried up the steps to her room. "I'm starving."

A minute later, she was back downstairs in sweatpants and a hoodie and heading for the kitchen, Luci right behind her. Kris plucked one of the triangular scones from the cooling rack and put it in her mouth, tilting her head as she contemplated it. The pink swirls from the raspberries that ran through the pastry gave the scone an aesthetically pleasing appearance that Luci was rather proud of.

"What do you think?" Luci asked, folding her arms and leaning against the counter.

"Hmm…" Kris chewed slowly. "It's not bad…"

"But not great?"

"I just feel like there's something a little off about the flavor balance," Kris grimaced. She glanced at the half-eaten scone. "I mean, I'm still going to eat the whole thing, but…what is it supposed to be? Just raspberry?"

"Raspberry and lemon."

"Yeah, I don't get any of the lemon."

"What?" Luci reached over her sister to grab one for herself. "I put a ton of it in there. Zest, too. There's no way you can't taste the lemon." She took a bite and chewed. "All right, so there *is* a way you don't taste the lemon. That's so annoying."

"It's just a balance thing," stated her sister. "You'll figure it out."

Luci grumbled. "I was trying to mess around with a scone recipe and make it mine," she frowned. "Apparently it's still got some ways to go."

"Uh-oh. You only hardcore experiment with recipes when something's wrong." Kris polished off the last of her scone and brushed off her hands. Little specks of crumb fell to the floor. Luci looked at them pointedly.

"Seriously? I just finished cleaning."

"Sorry. I'll get the broom. You know, for someone who is messy with literally everything, you sure like a clean kitchen."

"I'm not going to dignify that with a response," Luci called after her sister, who had ducked into a side room. A moment later, Kris reappeared with a broom.

After what happened over the summer, Kris had been a bit reclusive, staying a long time in her bedroom in the new house. It had only been in the past month or so that Kris had begun acting like her old self again. She had gotten a new job as an office manager and had finally started making jokes again. It was a slow process, but she was making strides, and Luci couldn't feel too down or defeated in her presence. Something about her just made everything seem a bit brighter.

"So, what's up?" Kris asked as she swept. "You only ever experiment with new recipes when you really need to think about something. Is it the skeleton?"

Luci'd told her sister already about finding the body and the mysterious room, but she hadn't gone into details. She'd only given the bare bones of the situation.

"Sort of." Luci told her about going back into the room, all the tools and how something had just felt off about the whole place.

"Well, considering there was a body there, I can't imagine that they would go back in there to collect things after the guy died," Kris pointed out. "It would make sense that they would just leave things there to avoid opening the door."

"But that would mean either our grandmother or grandfather or both knew about the body," Luci pointed out. "And I just have a hard time believing that they had something to do with someone's death."

"I know." Kris frowned. "That's bothering me, too. There's no way Grandma would ever kill anyone. She's too sweet for that. We don't know much about Grandpa, but do you really think he was capable of murder?"

"My guess is that they didn't know," Luci shrugged. "No idea how. Maybe Grandpa Joseph lost the key and someone used it? Killed the person, whoever they were, and locked the door after them. It would explain why someone mailed me the key if it were stolen."

"Maybe…" Kris replied, sounding a bit dubious. "What's your next step, then?"

"I want to know when that room was built," Luci reckoned. "If you ask me, it wasn't built with the rest of the library. If I can get my hands on the original blueprints, I'll be able to see if I'm right. I guess I'm going to go to the public records office and see if they might have them on file."

"Well," Kris surmised, "It's as good a plan as any."

"It's the only one I've got," Luci told her as she grabbed another scone and headed back to her room. "I need to go find out when the records office opens. Good night!"

***

The public records office was attached to the Town Hall, a pretty brick building with a clock tower rising above it. It was still early morning when Luci entered the small, slightly shabby room. Behind the counter were stacks of wooden file drawers and metal cabinets, some with pieces of paper sticking out. An older man was hunched in front of a computer with a pile of paper next to him. He muttered under his breath and paid Luci no mind as he clicked away, lost in his own world. The woman, who had to be about the same age as the man, smiled as Luci approached the counter.

"Hello, there," the woman greeted. "How can I help you?"

"Hi," she smiled warmly. "I'm Luci Mitchell, owner of the Mitchell Library?"

The woman behind the counter clapped her hands eagerly. "Of course," she exclaimed. "I thought you looked familiar. You look just like Annabelle."

"You knew my grandmother?" Luci asked, more than a little surprised.

The woman *hmmed* and tilted her head. "Not well, but I knew her by sight. I used to go to that library all the time when I was younger. She always had a kind word for everyone. I'm Suzanne, by the way."

"Pleasure. Anyway, I was hoping I could look at some of the old library blueprints. I wanted to check a couple of things."

Suzanne beamed, tapping a manicured finger on the counter. "Of course, dear! I'd be happy to help you."

Luci breathed. She'd thought it would be harder. "Fantastic! I–"

"We'll just need you to fill out Form 2E, which will allow us to fill out and file the A37. At that point, we'll be able to send you a 108. Then, all you'll need to do is a final CR3, and we'll be able to get it to you in about 5 to 10 business days."

Luci blinked. Had Suzanne even breathed while she said that? "Um, is there a way I don't have to do all that?"

"Not unless you want to fill out a Y14-C, and let me tell you, that one's a doozy. Plus, it takes twice as long to get the documents."

"Okay." She tried to hide her frustration. "Guess I better start on 2E."

"Of course! Now, if you could just fill out a G-1, I can get you that one."

She forced herself not to sigh.

***

By the time she returned to the library, it was close to ten. Patrick waved from behind the counter, and Simon fluttered over to her happily.

'Need food,' he told her, nipping her ear affectionately.

"Patrick, did you feed Simon?" Luci called, stroking the bird's chest.

"Of course I did." He pointed back toward the cage in her office. "You can see for yourself."

"You nasty little liar," Luci laughed, reaching a finger over toward the little beggar. Simon hopped on and Luci brought him to face her.

'Patrick liar,' Simon uttered. *'Need food.'*

Before Luci could respond, the door opened behind her. Simon looked over her head, squawked excitedly, then launched off Luci's finger to fly over to the newcomers. Luci turned, following Simon's trajectory as he fluttered over to Nick and sat on his head.

"Hey, Simon," Nick greeted his feathered friend. "How are you doing?"

'Patrick liar need food,' Simon told him. Luci hadn't realized until now that a bird could legitimately sound like it was complaining.

"Good thing I can fix that." Nick fished out a packet of apples and held it up. Beside him, Petra, his fiancé', gave Luci an apologetic look that said there was no stopping it. "Here you go."

"If you keep feeding him I'm going to ban you," Luci warned. The threat was hollow, and everyone, including Simon, knew it. "This is why he's obsessed with people food."

The parrot, ignoring his owner's objections entirely, took his prize of an apple slice and flew high up onto the window sill above the front door, where he knew Luci couldn't reach him and began eating.

"Sorry," Nick apologized, grinning widely.

Luci rolled her eyes but didn't bother griping at him anymore. She knew Nick well enough by now to know that he was never going to not give Simon treats whenever possible. She was fairly certain that Nick was Simon's second-favorite person behind her, and even that might be putting herself too high on the parrot's list.

Nick and Petra were also part of the book club, The Bookists. They'd been coming for years now. At one point, they'd had a regular meeting time. Nowadays, however, there never seems to be any rhyme or reason as to when they would show up. Nick and Petra, recently engaged, were two of the younger members, close to Luci's own age.

"What happened the other day, by the way?" Petra asked. "I came by to grab a book, but the doors were locked, and there were CSI trucks outside."

Luci sighed. She should have known they wouldn't be able to keep it quiet for long.

"There was a...complication opening that day," she hesitated.

"Not another body?" Nick's eyebrows shot up and were concealed by his brown hair.

Luci tapped the side of her nose. "I'm trying to keep this one a bit quieter," she voiced. "The last time was a little too public."

"What was too public?" Roger, another Bookist, asked as he appeared beside Nick.

'Skeleton in the library.' Simon, who had finished his initial snack, had swooped down to retrieve another treat from Nick.

Luci closed her eyes as Nick and Petra looked like they were holding back their laughter. So much for keeping it under wraps.

"A skeleton, really?" Petra asked once she'd gotten over her amusement at Luci's secret-spilling parrot.

"That's what it looks like," Luci replied. "Though I don't know anything else about it."

"Huh." Roger scratched his grey stubble as he contemplated the news. "Well, never a dull moment around here, eh?"

Luci tilted her head. "That's a rather mellow response, all things considered," she scoffed.

Roger shrugged. "By the time you turn 70, you've seen a few things."

"I can't imagine library skeletons are one of them," Luci half chuckled. Then his words got through to her. "70?" she asked. When Roger nodded, she continued, "So you were around when the library was built?"

He nodded. "Born and raised here. Dad was a miner, so was his dad."

Her pulse quickened in excitement. Maybe he would have some of the answers that she couldn't get from the library. "Do you remember anything strange about it?" she asked. "Or if there was any talk about more construction after the library was built?"

Roger chuckled. "You're giving my memory way too much credit, Luci," he winked. "I didn't come within a hundred feet of the library until I was nearly 40. The library was in full swing by then."

Luci huffed. It had been worth a shot, at least. She was starting to feel as if she didn't know the library at all. She'd spent most of her life playing in the aisles and the rest running the place. But the more she learned, the more she was starting to feel like she didn't know anything about the library at all.

"Oh, that's Elaine and Christine," Petra stated, gesturing to the two women, one in her thirties and the other middle-aged, pulling open the doors. "That's our cue. Vance said he was going to be late today."

"You can't actually think that talking about that dumpster fire of a book—which you hated, by the way—is more interesting than learning about a skeleton," Nick expressed. "I want to know more about—"

"Nope." Petra grabbed his arm, her chestnut hand standing out prominently against Nick's practically ghostly-pale skin. "Not our business."

She dragged Nick toward the two waiting women, and Roger followed. At one point, Petra looked over her shoulder to look at Luci and winked.

Luci watched them go, biting her lip as she was left alone with her thoughts again.

There has to be a way for her to learn more about the library. The only question was how?

Chapter 6

Chapter Six

T he kitchen was pleasantly warm, and the mouthwatering smells coming from the oven filled the air. There was already a plate of warm scones on the counter, steam still wafting lazily into the air, making Luci think of the pies in cartoons.

"You can definitely taste the lemon now," Kris murmured, her face puckering. "It gets into the back of your jaw."

"I don't think it's too much," chimed Rachel, Luci's best friend second only to Kris, as she tore a scone piece to pop blithely into her mouth." At an 'are you kidding' look from Kris, she swallowed before saying, "Okay, maybe a little."

Luci bit into one herself and was vexed to find out that her sister was right. Way too much lemon. This time it completely overpowered the raspberry.

"I think it's missing something," chimed in Sam, Luci's other best friend beside Rachel, as she craned for a closer sniff of her pastry, ever the discerning critic.

"Yeah, more raspberry to counteract the lemon," Kris suggested. For all her complaining, she had still eaten two of them already.

"No, not that." Sam shook her head, her light blond hair swishing with the motion. "It's missing something else. You've got two tart things in here."

"Raspberries aren't that tart," Luci protested.

"They are a bit. Anyway, I think adding something a bit sweeter might help with the balance. It's good as is, it just could be better."

"Any ideas on what?" Luci asked. The oven dinged, and this time she pulled out a tray of snickerdoodles.

"No clue," Sam responded cheerily. "You're the baker. You're supposed to be the one to figure that stuff out."

Luci stuck out her tongue, and Sam cackled.

"Why do I invite you guys over?" Luci teased.

"Because you love us," Rachel retorted with a cheesy grin. "And because if you didn't, you'd be forced to eat all of this by yourself. And I don't think *anyone* could eat this many sweets."

Sam nodded her agreement; it was true. Aside from Kris, Sam and Rachel were Luci's favorite people in the world. Rachel stood petite with luscious auburn locks cascading around her bright blue eyes, contrasting Sam's tall stature, fair hair, and warm brown eyes. They'd been friends for years after bonding over similar tastes in books and music. Sam and Rachel both worked in software development at the same company. Their busy schedules, especially over the past few months, had made it difficult to get to spend much time together. Now that time like this was a rare treat, Luci valued it immensely.

"Says the girl who ate the entire box of pralines I got her for her birthday in less than 24 hours," Luci retorted.

"And that's exactly why you need me." Rachel winked. "Who else are you going to have as a bottomless pit for all things sugar?"

A loud knock echoed through the house. The four women froze, then all looked at one another, perplexed.

"Did you order pizza without telling me so you could sneak it into your room and eat it all by yourself?" Luci asked Kris.

"That was one time. And no."

Unsure what to expect, Luci shrugged and made her way to the door. She could make out a figure behind the opaque window as she approached the door, though nothing definitive. Only as Luci drew near enough, could she discern a hazy orange smudge atop the silhouette behind the foggy glass of the entrance door, did she finally recognize the slight stoop in the familiar stature.

"Daniel?" she asked when she opened the door.

He was dressed far more casually than the last time she'd seen him in blue jeans and a t-shirt. It was actually a bit jarring to see him outside of the plain clothes he wore for work, his hands stuffed in his pockets as he gave a lazy smile.

"Hi, Luci," he grinned.

"Last time you made an unsolicited call to my house, you arrested my sister," Luci remarked. "So please tell me you're not here for that."

"No, I'm not," he promised. He looked past her, and without having to look, she knew that all three of the other women were peering in from the kitchen, trying to see what it was the detective wanted.

"Well, then." Luci stepped back, holding the door open so he could enter. "Do you want some scones? Or cookies?"

As if answering for him, his stomach growled loudly.

"I don't think I could ever turn down one of your baked goods," he confessed.

"You might," Kris called. "The scones are really lemony."

"I've been experimenting," Luci clarified.

"In that case, you've just found a very willing guinea pig." A hopeful smile graced Daniel's lips.

The two of them walked into the kitchen. Rachel, Sam, and Kris were sitting right where Luci had left them, all pretending that they hadn't been eavesdropping just seconds ago.

Plucking a scone from the tray, she held it out toward Daniel. "Here you go," she offered. He reached out for it, and Luci playfully retracted her hand, smirking slightly as she did. "Now, you tell me what you're doing here first, then maybe..." she wiggled the scone tauntingly.

Daniel gave her an amused look, slowly leaned down toward her, and plucked the scone from her hand before she could react. His eyes slightly rolled back, half closed as hers bulged in surprise, mouth unhinged. He winked, clearly pleased with himself until his smug expression changed as the tart lemon flavor hit. His eyes widened as he gagged, grunted, and finally cleared his throat, attempting to regain his composure.

"Told you it was lemony," Kris declared, and the women giggled.

"You weren't wrong," Daniel laughed once he'd swallowed. "Still good, though. Just not quite what I was expecting."

"The recipe still needs a bit of tweaking," Luci confirmed. "Serves you right for trying to work around a deal."

"I was going to tell you eventually," Daniel pointed out as he braved another bite. Not wanting another of Luci's scowls, he choked down his body's protests with minimal drama this round. Still, the twitch in his clenched jaw betrayed the battle waging, and his eyes flared noticeably enough to stir Luci's smile. "Otherwise, why would I be here?" he asked, once he managed to swallow.

"You're still skirting around the reason," Luci pointed out.

"All right, all right." He glanced around, eyes lingering on Kris, Sam and Rachel.

Luci, reading his mind, mentioned, "It won't be long until everyone in town knows about the skeleton and I'm sure you're not giving me privileged information. Besides, the guy's been dead for years, so I don't see how them knowing anything about it would jeopardize the case."

"Decades," Daniel corrected.

Luci tilted her head. "Sorry?"

"He's been dead for decades, not years."

Luci's eyes widened, her entire body straightening as realization raced through her. "Him? Not it. You found out who it is and when he died?" When Daniel nodded, Luci gave a small sigh of relief.

"I hate to admit it, but I'm kind of glad the guy's been dead for decades. It means I wasn't so oblivious as to not notice a murder taking place under my nose. Or feet, I guess."

"I don't know if you can claim not being oblivious," Daniel stated, eyes dancing as he gave a joking smile. "I mean, there was a body in your library for decades, and you never even realized."

"He's got a point," Kris agreed. Luci shot her a glare, and she shrugged. "I'm just saying, you're there all the time."

"I completely forgot about the door," Luci huffed, her annoyance mixing with sheepishness. "Eventually it just blended into the basement and I stopped noticing."

"Probably shouldn't go out for the detective's exam, then," Daniel teased. Luci narrowed her eyes and sneered playfully at him. He laughed. It was a deep, rich laugh, and Luci was surprised at how much she liked the sound of it. She looked down at the plate of cookies and grabbed one, hoping no one noticed the blush creeping up her face.

"Are you going to tell us the name or not?" Kris demanded.

"You and your sister are relentless, you know that, right?" There was no real grumbling behind Daniel's words. His tone was closer to fond amusement. "Yes. I want to know if you've ever heard of him."

"Why would we have heard of him?" Kris asked.

"He was found in my library," Luci answered for him. "In Grandma's library. Of course, there's a chance we could know him."

Daniel nodded. "I'm not expecting much, but I figured I had to give it a shot. Do either of you know anything about a man named William Fenton?"

The resounding silence and bemused expressions were answer enough. Luci's "No," was entirely unnecessary.

"He was a local who went missing here in the '80s," Daniel explained. "No one has seen or heard from him in decades."

Kris grumbled, "Guess we now know why.".

"How can you know who it was?" Rachel asked. It was a reasonable question. "It was a skeleton."

"You can still get DNA from skeletons," Sam chimed in. "It's just a bit harder."

"True," Daniel confirmed. "Unfortunately, though, not for this guy. He died way before the DNA database was established. The first use of DNA in criminal cases was 1986, so they wouldn't have had any of his on file to compare it to."

"Then how—?" Luci began, just as Daniel clipped in.

"You didn't notice it and I almost didn't, either. It turns out that the skeleton was missing a finger on one hand. A forensics team from Denver was able to do digital facial reconstruction pretty quickly. Though not an exact science, the pairing of those two elements provided the most likely identification."

"Neat," Sam exclaimed. "I should have gone into forensics. It sounds so cool."

"Better you than me." Luci gave an exaggerated shudder. "Seeing a couple dead bodies was enough for me. I don't need to be around them all the time at work."

"They do more than just that," Sam insisted.

"Still dealing with dead people all the time," responded Rachel.

The two of them devolved into a spirited, friendly argument about semantics and just how frequently forensic scientists have to investigate actual corpses. Daniel took the opportunity to walk over to Luci.

"Can I talk to you for a second?" he asked, his voice low. Something about his tone made Luci stiffen, the hairs on her arm and the back of her neck prickling uncomfortably. She glanced over at the other women. Kris had been roped into the forensics debate. None of them were paying her any attention.

"Alright."

She and Daniel walked into the living room, the din from her friends' spirited discussion subsided now that they were in another room.

"So, what's up?" Luci asked. "No takebacks. You can't go back on your word and arrest my sister now that you've gained access to my house. And sour scones."

She meant it as a joke, and she said it lightheartedly, however, her smile subsided when she saw Daniel's grim expression. "Oh boy," she cringed.

"How well did you know your grandmother?" he asked.

Luci forced herself to keep her composure despite the anxious knot that had abruptly formed and was now tightening in her chest. She could see red tinting the edges of her vision.

"Come on, Daniel," she pleaded, her voice hoarse. "Please don't ask that. You know she didn't have anything to do with it."

"There was a body in the basement of her library for over three decades by the time she died," Daniel reminded her. "That's more than a little suspicious. I have to look into her regardless of whether or not I believe you."

"She always told me it was Grandpa Joseph's room," Luci reflected. Then her eyes snapped back to Daniel. "If you so much as think about putting this on my grandfather who died in 1985 or something like that, then I'll have Simon poop all over your police car."

There was silence, punctured only by the conversation still going on in the kitchen. Luci and Daniel looked at one another for a long, pregnant moment.

Then they both burst into laughter. The knot unraveled.

"That definitely wasn't the threat I was expecting," Daniel grinned as he caught his breath. "It's definitely effective nonetheless. Luci, listen, I'm sorry I'm asking these questions at all. You know I wouldn't be doing my job if I didn't."

"Yeah," Luci sighed. "Look, you'll just have to take my word for it that my grandmother was the sweetest person. She couldn't harm a fly. Whatever happened down there, there was no way she was involved. What year did it happen, exactly?"

"He went missing in 1983."

Which, unfortunately, meant that her grandfather's involvement in the death was still up for debate. Luci hadn't known him well enough to give the same ringing endorsement she had given her grandmother.

"They're sure it's murder?" Luci asked. When the detective nodded, then she felt her stomach deflate like a balloon.

"Definitely a bullet wound, and considering there wasn't a pistol anywhere to be found..."

"My grandparents didn't have anything to do with any of it," Luci declared.

"You're probably right," Daniel sighed, pressing on. "However, until proven otherwise, I can't rule them out."

Luci could feel the anger boiling around inside her just below the surface. Before she was able to fight or argue, Daniel stepped toward her. He put his hand on her shoulder, his green eyes looking deep into Luci's own. There was something electric about his touch and as the current rushed through her, she found herself calming down.

"I'm just asking questions," he replied. "I promise I'm not jumping to conclusions, and I promise I won't make the same mistake I did last time."

It was one of the first times she had ever seen Daniel look this serious. The expression looked strange on his freckled face. His reassurance allowed her to back down, and the last of the fight ebbed out of her.

"Sorry," she murmured.

That easy grin of his was back. "It's all right." He stepped back, allowing his hand to fall from her shoulder. The pressure and warmth of his hand lingered. "I'd probably do the same if a detective who accused my sister of murder came asking about my grandparents in relation to a different murder."

"Well, you got there in the end last time. With my help of course."

Daniel laughed and tipped an imaginary hat. "And for that, I thank you immensely. I still have to find a way to thank you. Any suggestions?"

Something about the look in his eyes pulled Luci up short. There was a strange earnestness and sincerity to his expression that made it strangely difficult to know how to answer the question.

Eventually, she settled on, "You're a smart guy. I'm sure you'll think of something."

"You don't make it easy, do you?"

"Now, where's the fun in easy?" she asked.

Daniel chuckled, and some of that strange tension that had been brewing between them dissipated with the sound. Luci noticed her taut muscles relax only as the tension abated. Just then, a ding ruptured the mood. Daniel fished his phone out. "I've got to get going," he murmured, scrutinizing the screen.

"Case?" Luci asked.

"Nah. Pizza delivery." He winked. "Didn't think they'd be this quick. Or that you'd have food for me."

"Well, you can't let a good pizza go cold at your front step," Luci agreed. "Pretty sure that's a crime."

"If it isn't, it should be."

Daniel poked his head back into the kitchen and waved goodbye to the others as Luci waited to walk him to the front door.

"Take care of yourself, Luci," he told her, as he stepped across the threshold.

"You too. And promise me that you'll keep me posted on everything."

His head bobbed from side to side. "As much as I can, how's that?"

She pouted. "You never make it easy, do you?"

His grin turned radiant as it grew to spread across his face, matching that lively, mischievous glint in his eyes.

"Now, where's the fun in easy?"

Chapter 7

Chapter Seven

'*L*uci lost.'

Luci blinked, jumping slightly as she started. Simon was perched on the side of her desk, his head dancing from side to side as he looked at her.

'*Luci lost.*'

"Sorry, Simon," Luci whispered, stroking his back. "I guess I am a bit lost in my own world."

It was true. Ever since Daniel had stopped by her house the night before to ask about her grandmother, Luci's thoughts had been plagued with questions: about her grandmother, about her grandfather, about William Fenton. She couldn't stop wondering about how the missing man had ended up in her library. More importantly, she couldn't stop wondering if Daniel had been right and if her grandparents might have had something to do with Fenton's death. Occam's Razor stated that the simplest solution was often the correct one. In this case, the simplest solution was that her grandparents were involved. It had been their library after all. Except that didn't mesh with what she knew about her family.

She sighed and tried to bring herself back to the present. There was still so much work that she needed to do. She had to prep the library for winter now that things were getting cooler, and she needed to get the Halloween party organized and the details for it finalized. She also needed to balance the books and get a new volunteer to do story time for kids on Wednesdays.

Which might have been manageable were it not for the fact that she also needed to hire someone to help her and Patrick with all the work. She was feeling even more worn down and exhausted. How much longer could she go without another employee? Unfortunately, everyone she'd interviewed had been a nightmare. It was as if she were cursed to be unable to find a quality employee.

There'd been the teenager who had said she could work two shifts a month due to her schedule and had clearly thought that was more than enough to get hired. Then there was the older gentleman who she thought might be a good fit until he started leering at her during the interview. So far the worst had to be the college student who had given monosyllabic answers while looking at her phone and had then answered a call during the interview before proceeding to talk nonstop for a solid five minutes while Luci stared, dumbfounded. Eventually, she gave up and pulled up work on the computer, letting the girl finish her conversation, which lasted another ten minutes. Luci promptly showed her the door.

It was beginning to get to be too much, and she was fully aware of how tired she was. She didn't have time to dwell on who her grandparents really were or whether they had been involved in the death of a man she'd never heard of.

"I should leave it alone," she suggested to Simon. "It's a really, really bad idea for me to get involved. Daniel can take care of it. It'll make my life a lot easier, too. You know?"

Simon gave her a long, speculative look, his head bobbing as his eye regarded her.

'Luci liar.'

Luci stared at him for a long moment, then started laughing. Sometimes, Simon managed to get to the point better in two words than a poet could in an entire verse.

"Yeah, you're right," she confessed. "I'm definitely lying. Come on, then. Time to do some investigating."

Simon squawked excitedly and fluttered to her shoulder as she walked toward the door to the break room. He nuzzled against her, his dark beak rubbing against her cheek affectionately.

Making their way into the office, Simon stayed perched on her as she walked to her desk and booted up the computer. When the sluggish computer was finally up and running, she pulled up the browser, typing 'William Fenton' into the search bar and waited.

There were a lot of hits, and yet the William Fentons she came across in her search didn't fit the bill. Either they were older men who were still living, or they were far too young to be him. When she typed in William Fenton Juniper, Colorado, her luck started turning in her favor. It was an obituary for Patricia Cox, who had died a few years earlier. He was listed as a 'predeceased' relative, apparently her brother, along with her parents and a couple of other names. Luci scanned the list of 'survived by' names. Most were kids and grandkids. One, however, was listed as her sister, Sarah Myers.

Since Fenton wasn't working for any searches, she tried the living sister, a lifelong Juniper resident. There were a few nuggets of information scattered around the internet. One newspaper article in particular caught her eye. The article from two years ago showed her and a group of elderly women sitting together. It was a fluff piece about updates to a retirement home, and she was listed as a resident. Well, that was at least something, Luci thought.

Luci's continued searching didn't come up with much about Fenton himself. She even went so far as to look him up on a genealogy website, only finding a few documents that had him listed, though, nothing substantial answered any of her lingering questions.

She let out an irritated huff of air and slumped back in her chair. It was rare that the internet let her down. She couldn't figure out what she was missing, or rather than what the *internet* was missing.

Because he vanished in the '80s, dummy, a voice in her head told her.

She snapped her fingers. Regardless of how rude her inner voice was (she didn't think the dummy was particularly necessary), it had a point. If it were in the '80s, there probably wasn't much information on him on the internet. She needed another way to gather information.

Luci berated herself for overlooking the obvious - she should have begun rifling through those vintage newspapers first. It had been ages since anyone had requested ancient copies of *Juniper Times*, the local paper, and their newspaper collection had completely slipped her mind. She had been meaning to digitize it for a while but hadn't gotten around to it yet.

Now, as she was pulling out the long drawer where the newspapers were lined out neatly, she was starting to wish she had.

The pages were yellow and brittle, even so, they were still in good enough condition to handle. At least Luci knew that Fenton had gone missing in '83, which gave her a place to start. That was still 365 papers she would have to sort through. Her cheeks puffed out before she slowly released her breath. Luci surmised it was better than the thousands she would have had to scan otherwise.

Before she went through each paper individually, she skimmed the front pages. Juniper wasn't particularly big, and not a lot happened. There was a good chance that a missing person would make the front page.

Mercifully, she was right. On June 20th, there was a side article on the front page titled: Local Man Still Missing.

The police are still searching for any leads that might direct them to William Fenton, who went missing on June 3rd of this year.

That was all she needed. She took the paper and then grabbed the June 3rd and 4th papers. She scanned the rest of 1983 to see if there were any other pieces that mentioned him on the front page. Any further mention of Fenton, if it existed, didn't make front page news.

She could table the search for more on Fenton later. Right now, finding something physical felt hopeful. These old newspapers might reveal clues not tied to her grandparents. She breathed deeply to steady her nerves as she shut the long drawer.

When she got back to her office, she spread out the first paper with the missing person announcement splashed across the front page.

The police are still searching for any leads that might direct them to William Fenton, who went missing June 3rd of this year.

Fenton, 33, has lived in Juniper his entire life. Over the years, thanks to his charity work and his dedication to make Juniper the best place it could possibly be, Fenton has become a beloved member of the community.

Sources close to the investigation have said, under the promise of anonymity, that officials are no closer to finding him than they had been when he was first reported missing by his fiancé, Margaret Stinson, a little over two weeks ago. His last sighting was when he left work early due to a migraine. His second-in-command, Larry West, said that migraines are not uncommon for Fenton, who owns the Fenton Construction Company.

Police and Fenton's family are urging anyone who knows anything to come forward at this time.

She read and reread the article, desperately hoping for new insight or revelation. To her disappointment, the writing failed to drop additional clues or shed further light on her ongoing investigation. None of the other papers gave her any new information until she found an expanded piece that ran after the initial article with one big addition: a photo...

Fenton reminded Luci of a ferret, though not necessarily in an unappealing way. His features were unconventional, with a crooked nose, long face, and a hat that was clearly trying to conceal premature baldness. The smile he was flashing at the camera was one she could tell had broken hearts in his youth. It lit up his entire face in a charming way that blended the otherwise disjointed features. She stared at it, trying to connect the picture of the man in the photo to the skeleton she had found in the library's basement. She couldn't reconcile the two in her mind.

Besides the photo, the most information she could gather was that he owned a construction agency and he also did a lot of charity work. Nothing indicated that he had been involved in anything dangerous or unsavory that might have led to his death. There was also nothing connecting him to the library or her grandparents.

She slumped backward, groaning as she rubbed her face. She glared at the newspaper as if her glower would terrify it into revealing its hidden secrets. Her intense gaze failed to extract any secrets from the inanimate paper.

She felt the frustrating nagging sensation that she was missing something once again. Some piece she overlooked was surely the next breadcrumb, offering clues about just how tangled her family might be in Fenton's decades-old fate. If Luci could uncover this elusive lead, it may help direct her next step in unraveling the generations-long mystery broiling beneath her beloved library's floorboards.

The only problem was that she had absolutely no idea what was eluding her.

Chapter 8

Chapter Eight

J uniper Fields Retirement Home was a beautiful brick building with a pristine lawn. When Luci walked inside, the lobby was clean and pleasant music was playing softly through the speakers. A group of men were hunched over in the sitting room past the reception desk, and she could see playing cards in their hands. Another couple was sitting curled on a couch watching something on TV. It all seemed rather quaint and cozy. Cream colored walls were covered in inoffensive, generic paintings and photos. Luci's boots click-clacked on the amber-colored ceramic tile as she approached the desk, cutting through the quietness of the building.

"Hi, I'm here to see Sarah Myers," Luci told the woman manning the reception desk.

After her semi-successful-but-not-really research into Fenton, she had only one solid lead - his sister at the retirement home. Luci was unsure of what useful insights she could offer but felt compelled to try this approach. The alternative meant returning to scour that extensive drawer yet again. She chose the former.

The orderly behind the counter looked up at her, regarding her politely through large glasses. She smiled cautiously before bending over to glance at the computer.

"It doesn't look as though she has any restrictions on visitors," the woman remarked, more to herself than to Luci.

"I called yesterday. She should know I'm coming." When Luci had called the nursing home asking to speak to Sarah, she wasn't sure how best to approach the situation. What would get her to open up to a complete stranger? By now, Daniel would have told her they'd found her brother's body, so she wasn't worried about delivering bad news. It felt too disingenuous to pose as a reporter or some other position of authority, so in the end, the truth felt like the best option: she was an interested party and had a few questions to ask. She hadn't been sure it would work and was thrilled it did the trick.

After calling Sarah's room to confirm that she was indeed expecting a visit from one Luci Mitchell, the orderly smiled and nodded.

"She's in room 313," she indicated with a slight tilt of her head. "Elevator is down the hall and to the left."

Luci smiled her appreciation and then followed the instructions. The halls were all carpeted in a red and gold pattern and the walls were all the same uniform cream, with identical lights spaced evenly apart. It all looked so similar that she nearly got lost on the short trip. Nevertheless, she made her way through the corridors as the golden letters on the apartment doors indicated she was headed in the correct direction. In less than five minutes after talking to the orderly, she was knocking on room 313.

The plump woman who opened the door looked like the older, feminine version of the photograph she'd seen of Fenton in the paper. Her smile had the same effect as her brother's, radiating warmth that instantly put Luci at ease.

"You must be Luci," she greeted. "Please, come in, come in."

The small apartment behind the door was lovelier than Luci had imagined it would be. The carpeted living room was open and spacious, with a small kitchen in one corner. The sliding glass doors on the far side of the apartment opened onto a tiny balcony with a handful of potted plants and a wicker chair with a plush green cushion. The walls were adorned with family photos while the shelves were dotted with knick-knacks that gave the place a cozy, personal touch. It was the perfect size for an elderly woman on her own.

"Thank you for meeting with me." The plush couch hugged Luci as she sat down. "I'm sorry about your loss."

Sarah's face fell slightly as she sat in the armchair across from her guest. "I mourned Will a long time ago," she breathed. "After over thirty years, you start to give up hope. It was sad, indeed. Nevertheless, I'm glad to have closure, although it left so many questions. I have no idea what he was doing in your library."

Luci gaped, a brief feeling of panic slamming into her. She almost bolted right then. How had she known? When Luci had spoken to Sarah on the phone, she had only said she was an interested party. She hadn't mentioned the library at all.

At Luci's stunned expression, Sarah gave a knowing, slightly smug smile. "Detective Flinn told me that his body was found at Mitchell Library. Your last name is Mitchell. It doesn't take a genius, dear."

"Right." Luci coughed awkwardly. She really should have guessed that one. "Um, yeah. That's my library."

"Were you the one who found him?" When Luci nodded, Sarah continued, "I can't imagine how hard that had to be for you."

"It was definitely a shock," Luci admitted. "I was hoping I could get some answers to help make sense of it."

"Of course." Sarah smiled fondly. "Go ahead and ask away."

"What can you tell me about your brother?"

"Oh, William was a great man." Sarah smiled wistfully, clearly soaring on an old memory. "He was a good big brother. Always made sure he had time for me, even when he pretended to hate me. He'd grumble about having to take me somewhere, and yet, he'd still always buy me ice cream on our way home."

"What about when he was older?"

Sarah grunted, her bones popping as she adjusted herself in her seat. "Up until maybe a year or two before he vanished, nothing much had changed between us. Although, he had started to get cagey and evasive. I tried talking to him about it, but he always said I was imagining it and that I didn't know what I was talking about." She gave a throaty laugh. "Almost had me convinced I was wrong. Until he disappeared."

"And you think it had something to do with him being *cagey*?"

"His disappearance? I can't say for certain. I thought it was a solid theory, though. That's one of the things the police always ask you: *were they acting any differently?* For all I know he could have been worried about money and that was why he was so strange. Despite that, it might have just been a coincidence."

"Money?" Luci tilted her head.

"I loved my brother, rest his soul, but he was never any good with money. He'd tell you himself...he just loved to give it all away - even if it was just a little bit. It's a wonderful trait and I admired him for it. Unfortunately, it brought along with it some financial problems there toward the end. He would always pick up odd jobs whenever he got the chance, and that kept him afloat, sure. Admittedly, he did a lot of things pro bono as well."

"So by the time he disappeared, he was not doing well financially?"

"He didn't discuss finances with me regularly," Sarah admitted. "However, his clothing was... on the shabby side around the time he disappeared. I figured that was the reason he was acting a bit strange – he'd had his share of ups and downs because he was always there to help others. Though I doubt anyone realized he may have needed help himself."

Luci thought about how to ask the next question delicately. "You don't think he might have gotten involved with some...unsavory people, do you?"

Sarah laughed. "Are you kidding? Of course not. Will was never the type of person to go in with someone like that."

Luci bit her tongue. She wanted to point out that there was always a chance she didn't know her brother as well as she thought she did. Some people tended to have big secrets they kept hidden, especially from family. Luci didn't think that would go over particularly well. And besides, wasn't she trying to prove that about her grandparents? Who was she to say Sarah was wrong? She certainly knew her brother when he died far better than a woman who hadn't even been alive at the time of his disappearance.

Luci was beginning to realize that she wasn't getting anywhere with her line of questioning. She was no closer to finding the answers she came looking for, and she was running out of questions.

"Do you have any idea what he might have been doing at the library?"

Sarah shook her head, smiling sadly. "I've been asking myself that question since that detective came to visit me. I did not know the owners - presumably your parents or grandparents - particularly well. When Detective Flinn asked me if I knew of any connection between Will and the library, I couldn't come up with anything. I still can't. It doesn't make any sense."

"No kidding," Luci said, sighing. "I wish I had some answers."

Sarah gave her a sympathetic look. "I can imagine," she related. "I wish I could help, dear. I have just as many questions as you do, I'm afraid. I have no idea what he was doing at the library, or who might have wanted to kill him or why. Believe me, if I knew anything, I would tell you in a heartbeat."

The worst part was that Luci believed her. "I understand. Thank you. If I learn anything, I promise to let you know."

Luci left, frustrated and feeling as though she was no closer to the truth than she was before shuffling through old newspapers. She hadn't gained anything from the meeting aside from a pleasant conversation. There was no apparent connection with Fenton to the library, and she didn't discover anything that might prove her grandparents weren't involved with his murder. She was back at square one.

She walked through the halls, then stopped, frowning as she looked around. The place had dozens of meandering corridors. Luci realized she had gotten turned around at some point since stepping off of the elevator. Unsure how it happened, she now failed to spot any familiar landmarks leading back to the front desk. She must have unknowingly taken the hallway as she mulled about the lingering questions and feelings of time wasted. Slightly exasperated with herself, Luci breathed deeply to focus, certain she could retrace her steps.

"Great," she muttered. Looking down the corridor that resembled all of the others, Luci shrugged and chose a direction.

"Annabelle?"

Luci pulled to a halt and spun toward the voice. It had been a tired, quavering voice. For a moment, she wondered if she'd heard correctly. Craning her head back to peer into the open room, she saw an old woman sitting in bed, her eyes locked on Luci.

"Annabelle," the woman repeated.

Another woman peered around the door. Her short brown hair was cut in a bob, accentuating her pixie-like features. She studied Luci with polite curiosity that also felt somehow cold.

"Annabelle, dear," the elderly woman in the bed called out weakly. Her wrinkled face creased even further when she smiled. "It's so good to see you. It's been too long. How is Joseph? I'm so glad I ran into you. There's something I need to talk to you about."

Annabelle? Joseph? The bottom of Luci's stomach seemed to vanish as she stared in mute bewilderment. The woman was talking about her grandparents. No, more than that, she thought Luci *was* her grandmother.

"I'm Luci," she told her as she stepped closer to the doorframe. "Annabelle was my grandmother. How did you know her?"

The woman frowned, her brow wrinkling in confusion. "You're not Annabelle?" she asked.

The younger woman stood from where she'd been sitting and stepped in front of Luci, blocking her view. She was wearing a nurse's outfit.

"I'm really sorry," the nurse stated. "She's a bit confused."

"No, th-that's my grandmother she's talking about," Luci protested.

The woman hesitated, biting her lip as she looked behind her.

"I'm *really* sorry about that," she lowered her voice, as she stated her apology again.

"Do you mind if I speak to her?" Luci asked as the woman already started shaking her head.

"No, I'm sorry. She needs rest. She's not in a good spot at the moment. And since you're not family, I can't let you in."

Luci wanted to argue, though she could see in the other woman's face that there was no yielding on her end.

"I understand," Luci resigned. "I apologize for trying to butt in."

The woman nodded, smileless, then stepped back into the room, closing the door as she did. It was as blatant a dismissal as she could give without slamming the door.

Luci stared at the closed door for a long moment, her thoughts swimming. She'd always been told that she resembled her grandmother when she was younger. Hearing she bore an uncanny resemblance to that historical image proved worlds apart from a stranger actually mistaking Luci for her grandmother in the flesh.

She wanted to know more. She wanted to bang on the door and talk to the woman if only to learn more about her grandmother. Too bad the woman's nurse had made it perfectly clear that she wasn't welcoming any questions at the moment.

Swallowing her disappointment, she sauntered down the hall, meandering the corridors. As she wandered aimlessly, her thoughts were consumed by the mysterious old woman behind that door. Curiosity consumed Luci - who was this woman and how did she know her grandmother? The questions followed each hurried step as she found herself striding past the front desk and out the exit, preoccupied and still lacking any answers several minutes later.

Chapter 9

Chapter Nine

Luci had never realized just how cramped her grandmother's handwriting was until she had to squint over it to determine if that vertical line was supposed to be a 1 or a 7. The faded ink and old, yellowing pages didn't help with the task. Her mood wasn't helped by the fact that she had several more identical leather-bound ledgers stacked to her right, awaiting her attention. It was a little after closing, and Luci was leaning over the circulation desk, hunched over the books, looking for answers she wasn't even sure existed.

A rustling of wings informed her that Simon had glided over to perch beside her. He waddled into the corner of her vision, head tilting as he regarded the pages. He bent, flicked the pages with his beak, then looked at Luci.

'It's paper,' he said.

"That's right," Luci replied, stroking his head, her eyes still glued to the manuscript. "Books are made of paper." Over the last several years since she'd taken ownership of Simon, she'd been trying to teach him different materials—paper, rock, plastic, metal, wood, glass and the like. Now, when he was bored, he would fly around nibbling on things or flicking his beak against them, before proudly declaring the desk was wood or that the bars on his cage were metal.

'Snack?' he squawked hopefully.

Luci rummaged around in what she thought of as the 'bird drawer' and pulled out a bag of parrot cookies.

"I knew you were a hypocrite," a voice called triumphantly. Luci glanced up to see Kris heading toward her from the front entrance, sandy-colored hair bouncing behind her as she came toward the desk. "You always complain about other people giving Simon food, and here you are, shamelessly giving him treats just because he asked."

"The difference is in how much," Luci retorted as Simon plucked the little cookie from between her fingers and soared away ecstatically. "There has to be some regulation."

"Talk, talk, talk, that's all you are."

"What are you doing here, anyway?" Luci asked. "It's after closing."

Kris raised an eyebrow as she leaned over the desk. "I was coming to meet my sister for dinner like we agreed last night. I've been thinking about Juniper Brewery's pizza all day. I'm starving."

Luci stared, her mind blank. Then she remembered and she groaned, slamming the heel of her palm against her forehead. "Oh, god, I'm so sorry. I completely forgot."

"I figured you had forgotten. The fact that you'd locked the library and I had to get in with my key gave me a clue. Everything alright? You're usually not this spacey."

"I got distracted. Lot on my plate right now."

"Yeah, I get it. No worries. Whatcha up to, then, if not getting ready for pizza?"

"Looking up info on Grandma and Grandpa," Luci shared. "I've been going through some of these old records." She gestured at the books strewn across the table. "These are all old financial records and ledgers from the first few years the library was open."

"Wait, the ledgers from the '70s and '80s are still around?"

"Yup." Luci held up the ledger in her hand and waggled it. "Looks like I'm not the only one in the family who has issues throwing things out. Besides, these types of things are useful for the future. I expected they would have stuff like this. This was in an old filing cabinet back in storage; there are *lots* of cabinets back there. I figured they kept everything."

"Bragging about being from a family of hoarders isn't really something a lot of people do," Kris teased.

Luci rolled her eyes.

"Anything in particular you're looking for?"

"Anything I can find." Luci rubbed her eyes. "My eyes are killing me from staring, though."

"You're just getting one step closer to completing your librarian-ification. First shushing people all the time, then glasses, then a bun."

"The only person I shush regularly is you." Luci poked Kris playfully. "And that's because you insist on gasping loudly and telling everyone around you when you come to a good twist in a book."

"That was one time!"

"Twice."

"Agree to disagree?" Kris held up a Vulcan salute.

Luci chuckled, slumping as she raised a reciprocal Vulcan salute.

With a big toothy grin, Kris asked, "Find anything interesting?"

Luci's brow furrowed as she looked down at the ledger. "I'm not sure," she admitted. "There is one thing, though. I don't know what to make of it."

"What?"

She pointed to a section in the ledger that was over to her left. "This one is from the '70s when the library was built. It looks like they put a lot of money into the library to get it up and running. Like, a lot a lot."

"So?"

"Well, if these are correct, then they were in the red for the entirety of the '70s," Luci stated. "If you ask me, they were probably living off savings or Grandpa's job. However, this ledger—" and she pointed at the ledger in front of her, the one she'd been furiously studying when Kris had come in. "—from '82 tells a completely different story. All of a sudden, revenue skyrockets."

"Weird," Kris uttered, leaning over. "Maybe the library finally got popular?" Things like this take a while to get off the ground. Maybe it took Grandma some time to get used to it. Running a business isn't easy."

"Maybe..." Luci muttered. She bit her lip, looking down at the numbers. "Kris, if I didn't know any better, I would say this looks like money laundering."

Kris stared as if doubting what she was hearing. "You can't be serious," she breathed.

"I wish I weren't," Luci replied. "Maybe I'm just imagining things. I can't imagine either of them doing something like that. It's ridiculous. Where would the money they were laundering be coming from anyway?"

Kris picked up one of the ledgers and studied it curiously. Then shook her head. "It's gotta be something else."

"I hope so." The words came out more earnestly than Luci had expected. Her grandmother had helped raise her and Kris. She had countless fond memories of her. How they used to play hide and seek around the library, or how she had taught Luci to read. She had even been the one to introduce Luci to baking. Whenever she was over at Grandma's while her mother was working, Grandma Annabelle would teach her how to bake from scratch. "Nothing from a box," her grandmother would sniff.

The thought that Annabelle could have been doing something illegal, or could have somehow been involved in Fenton's death was entirely incongruous with the woman Luci had known. Luci was not about to let her grandmother's reputation become tarnished, or her own memories sullied. Even though Luci hadn't known her grandfather, she was certain Grandmother Annabelle wouldn't have married someone unsavory. She wouldn't let either of them be accused of any misdoings...not on her watch.

If she found evidence stating otherwise, Luci bit her lip. She didn't want to think about that possibility.

The problem was that the ledgers potentially provided exactly what she had feared most.

"How's hiring going?" Kris asked. She was clearly attempting to distract Luci from her concerns over their grandparents.

It worked.

Luci grimaced and gave a melodramatic *ugh*. "Awful," she voiced. She'd had two more interviews since Darren, and both of them had been disastrous. "Last woman I interviewed said she believed banned books were banned for a reason, and all copies ought to be burned. I mean, why on earth apply to work in a library if you believe *that*?"

"Maybe she wanted to help set them on fire?" Kris suggested. The two of them looked at one another, a bubble of laughter caught in their throats, erupting irrepressibly into convulsive guffaws that made them both double over clutching their stomachs.

"That's got to be it," Luci quipped, chuckling, wiping the tears from her eyes.

"Don't worry," Kris assured her, "You'll find someone."

"Are you sure I can't convince you to come work for me temporarily?" Luci begged.

"No, thank you." Kris shook her head emphatically. "You aren't roping me into cleaning Simon's birdcage every day."

"It's not *every* day," Luci responded coyly. "Every other day at the most."

"I gotta say, I really like my job 'cause I don't have to put up with customers and their complaints every day," Kris remarked. Reaching over, she closed the open ledger in front of Luci. "Now come on. You need a break and pizza's calling. Nothing good is going to come from staring at the ledgers unless you're trying to hit your quota for max stress points on your phone. Unless you magically plan on traveling back in time to find the answers, pizza is in your future."

Luci opened her mouth to protest, then sighed. Kris was probably right. She'd been thinking so much about what must have happened all those years ago to no avail. It had been like banging her head against the wall for a week straight. She needed a break.

As if to emphasize the point, her stomach growled loudly. Kris didn't even try to hide her snicker.

"Let me get Simon back into his cage," Luci said.

As the sisters locked up together, Kris chatted about the pizza toppings she planned to pair with a movie night as they made their way to Brewery's. Despite Luci nodding absentmindedly at Kris' suggestions, Luci barely registered her sister's words, her thoughts already wandering far from their familiar rituals of comfort. It was back in the library, with the ledgers on the circulation desk. They were telling her a story, alluding to something big that she knew would help her make sense of everything and figure out why Fenton's bones were now coming back to the living.

Chapter 10

Chapter Ten

"See you, Patrick," Luci called out, waving as her only employee strolled out the door. "Thanks for coming in."

Patrick waved behind him to acknowledge he'd heard, then vanished as he descended the steps outside and out of view. A minute later, she walked around the circulation desk to lock everything up. Outside, long shadows and golden light signaled the sun setting.

The library was closed. She should get home. However, Luci felt the tug of unfinished business urging her to stay. Her mind was still swimming with all the bizarre and disjointed information she'd collected over the past couple of days since taking a break with Kris. She had been trying and failing to make sense of it ever since her talk with Sarah, but it felt like the answer continued to elude her. It was driving her mad, and she wanted nothing more than to uncover the truth. The only problem was she had no idea where to go next. The thought of going home, where she would have nothing to do but dwell on those unresolved thoughts that had plagued her ever since discovering those bones, filled her with dread.

'Luci leave' Simon flew over and landed on the edge of the circulation desk as she walked out of her office.

She chewed on her lip, mulling over the parrot's question. Meanwhile, Simon watched her, shifting his weight from foot to foot, his wings fluttering slightly as if he was considering launching into the air again.

Then it hit her. Another avenue that she hadn't fully explored yet. Wasn't there an entire room filled with items that might give her some answers? A certain room that was more or less a time capsule? What if the answers were tucked away with Fenton's body, buried somewhere amidst the jumbled chaos of clues - a puzzle so tangled not even the police could unravel it?

"Not just yet," she mumbled, digging her gloves out of the drawer where she'd dumped them after she'd last used them. "I've got to make a stop in the basement."

Simon squawked excitedly.

'Go to basement.'

Before she could argue or tell him he should stay up here, Simon took off, flying overhead in the direction of the basement door. Luci sighed and rubbed her temples.

"One of these days I'm getting you a leash," she called after him.

The only response she got was a joyous, *'Basement come Luci.'*

Any attempt to stop the bird from swooping into the basement the instant she opened the door would have been futile. She grumbled under her breath as Simon landed on her head, his talons digging gently into her scalp as he adjusted his position. Perched solemnly, the parrot looked on as she unlocked and pulled open the basement door.

The basement looked the same as it always had. The same strings turned on the lights; the same steps creaked ominously as she descended; the same hot water heater sat in the corner next to the same breaker box, yet everything felt different. Finding the corpse had transformed the basement mood, casting an ominous pall, evident in the shiver it sent down her spine. Now that she was down here, she realized that she had been avoiding the basement altogether since her last exploration of the now-unlocked room. She repressed a shudder and forged ahead.

The light in her grandfather's old room clicked on, showing Luci the cluttered shelves. This time, though, the curios and boxes promised possible answers. They instilled a new air of excited curiosity, rather than an ominous vibe felt just moments ago. For the first time since she'd discovered the room, she didn't feel on edge.

"Any idea where to start?" she asked Simon, who was still contentedly resting on her head.

'Start.'

"Very helpful." She reached up to stroke the bird and felt him lean into the touch. "It's going to take a week to go through all this."

'Start.'

Taking Simon's sage advice, she started. She grabbed the stepladder that had been resting near the water heater and clambered up to reach the old boxes on the top shelf. The smell of must and mildew was so pungent that she started sneezing violently.

Once her body stopped convulsing from the microbe invasion, she began pulling down boxes. By the time she wrapped her hands around the flimsy corner of the second box, she felt grateful she'd thought to grab her gloves, their barrier keeping layers of filth from coating her skin. Even though she knew logically that couldn't feel the grime through the fabric, she could still sense it on her fingers and palms, like phantom spiderwebs.

She pulled down three boxes and peeked inside. The first one had old toys inside, everything from an ancient China doll to a ball glove to an old-school Barbie. The second one was filled with old family memorabilia and had a box that, when she opened it, was filled with photos. The third was more of the second, and as Luci began rummaging deeper in the boxes, she pulled out the items, laying them out and arranging them as she studied each piece. The more she pulled out and arranged by the significance of whether or not it was a potential clue, she began to get more and more disheartened. She questioned if her time down there was an exercise in futility with a side of no answers here.

"Do you think this was a stupid decision?" Luci asked Simon, now perched on an edge of a box, who simply cocked his head at her. "You know what? Don't answer that." She groaned as she looked at the items splayed out around her in a circle. At that moment, Luci felt as if her search for answers had been a stupid endeavor. "Regardless, I can't sit on this floor anymore."

Still unwilling to give up on the venture entirely, despite her wavering negative thoughts, she scooped up a box of items she hadn't gone through yet and headed upstairs.

Once she was back in the cool ambiance of the library, Luci took a deep cleansing breath, as she pulled out the items and spread them out as best she could on the circulation desk. She hunched over, looking at the pieces, trying to decipher if any of them might give her some insight into her grandparents' involvement with William Fenton.

Simon perched precariously on the edge of the box once again, forgoing his usual placement on Luci. His head tilted, beady eye focusing on something Luci couldn't see.

"Don't you dare—" she began. Too late. Before the final word was out of her mouth, Simon's head had darted into the box, vanishing temporarily before reappearing with a photo speared on the end of his beak.

"Simon, give me that—"

Simon, apparently deciding that his owner had said *Simon, please fly off with the photo and remain just out of reach as I try to catch it*, launched into the air when her hand was mere centimeters from snatching back the photo.

She could have just let him fly off with his prize, but she didn't know if an old-timey photo had some chemical on it that might be dangerous to him. Even though the odds were small, it wasn't a risk she was willing to take.

Which, of course, resulted in a chase around the library. Simon was having the time of his life, soaring from aisle to aisle. Luci, meanwhile, was getting progressively out of breath.

"Simon," she begged, after maybe five minutes of this. By now, they were in the far corner of the second floor, near the biographies. "Please just give me the photo."

Simon cocked his head as if considering. Then he gingerly dropped the photo on top of the shelf, far out of her reach.

'Food?' he asked.

Luci stared. "Are you...extorting me?"

'Food,' he repeated, bobbing his head up and down as if nodding.

"I'm not giving you food for a photo," she snorted.

Simon's response to the declaration was to pick the photo up again and fly away.

It was another five minutes of running after him until Luci finally conceded, "All right, all right. Food for the photo."

Instantly, Simon glided over to her, landing on her arm, and deposited the photo in her hand.

'Food now,' he demanded, waddling up her arm to her shoulder.

Luci barely heard him. She was too fixated on the photo in her hand. The top was mangled slightly from where Simon had been holding it captive in his beak. Luckily, the people in the image were still clear as day.

One of them was her grandfather, tall and well-built, with sandy-brown hair similar to Luci's. He was smiling at the camera, his arm slung around the other person in the photo. The other man was unmistakably William Fenton.

He had the same smile as he'd had in the newspaper. There was no doubt who it was. Here was undeniable proof that her grandfather and Fenton had known one another.

With trembling hands, she flipped the photo over. 'August 1982' was scribbled in pen across the back. This had been taken less than a year before Fenton had gone missing.

"They'd known one another," Luci breathed. If they had known one another as the photo indicated, then the odds that her grandparents had somehow been involved in his death had just skyrocketed. The thought formed a knot of confusion and unease to tighten in her chest.

She took just long enough to give Simon a couple of parrot cookies—she always kept her word when it came to promising Simon food—then ran back to the box where he'd found the photo.

The top of the box that had been holding the photos had gotten dislodged when she'd carried it up from the basement. She had dismissed them when she first saw them, assuming they were just old family pictures. She was wrong, it was more than just family memories.

She thumbed through the pictures, looking for anyone or anything unusual, or any more photos of Fenton.

At first, there was nothing, the photos turned out to be exactly what she'd initially predicted: family memories. They were interesting, for sure. She enjoyed glimpsing the photos of her grandparents in Hawaii, while several others of them showed the early stages of work on the library. Witnessing the historic change from what it had looked like in the beginning to what it was now felt unreal. It was hard to imagine she was standing in the same building.

She was beginning to get discouraged when mid-flip she found another photo of Fenton. Based on the familiar mountaintop view in the background and the ski gear, it had been taken over at the ski slopes on the edge of town. That wasn't what pulled her up short. It was the woman next to him, the one he had his arm wrapped around as they smiled happily at the camera.

It was difficult to be certain—forty years was a long time, after all. There was something familiar about the woman that made Luci look closer. If she didn't know any better, she could have sworn it was the woman from the retirement home. The one who had called her Annabelle.

"Who are you?" Luci asked the photograph. "And what do you have to do with William Fenton?"

Chapter 11

Chapter Eleven

T he next morning, Luci strolled into the Juniper Police Department with a cup of coffee in each hand and a tub of homemade pastries tucked beneath her arm. The receptionist pointed her in the direction she needed to go, and a moment later, she was knocking on the side of Detective Daniel Flinn's desk with her shoe.

Daniel looked up. Surprise was quickly replaced with a pleased expression.

"Please tell me one of those is for me?" he asked, nodding toward the coffees.

"What? No, hello, how are you?" she teased.

"Hello, how are you? Please tell me one of those is for me?"

"Much better. And yes. As are these." She placed one cup in his outstretched hand, then put the Tupperware on the tidy desk. "Don't worry, these aren't the scones. Just your basic chocolate chip cookie and croissant bribe."

"My favorite kind of bribe." Daniel took a sip of coffee and groaned in satisfaction. "Thanks. Now, to what do I owe the pleasure? I can't imagine you're bribing me without an ulterior motive."

"You got me there," admitted Luci. She sat down in the chair next to his desk and pulled the photos out of her purse. "I came to show you this. I found it last night while I was going through some of the boxes in the basement."

She handed him the one of Fenton and her grandfather first. Daniel studied the photograph for a second, then his eyebrows shot up.

"Is that your grandfather?" he asked. When Luci nodded, he said, "I thought you said Fenton didn't have any connection to the library."

"Apparently, I was wrong."

He frowned, flipping it over, taking note of the date, then flipping it back to consider the photo again. "You know what this implies, right?" he asked.

"Oh, trust me. I'm very aware of what it implies. And I don't like it. However, that's not all." At Daniel's inquisitive look, she handed over the second photo. "I've seen the woman before. Or at least, I think I have."

He looked at her sharply, every bit the detective. "Where?"

"Juniper Fields Retirement Home." She told him briefly about her trip there, and her encounter with the woman.

"I should've known you would go there if you found out about Sarah," Daniel remarked.

"Any idea who this woman is?" she asked.

"I'm not sure." He sighed, pushing away from the desk and standing as he grabbed his coffee. There's one way to find out. Whose car are we taking?"

"Mine looks like a tornado ran through it. So probably yours."

"In that case..." He took a sip of coffee and smacked his lips, before making an overly exaggerated *after you* gesture. "Let's get going."

***

When they arrived at Juniper Hill, Daniel flashed his badge and gave the orderly at the desk a winning smile.

"I'm Detective Flinn," he began. "We're looking for the woman in..." he glanced over his shoulder at Luci.

"122," Luci chimed in, after briefly closing her eyes and remembering the golden number.

The orderly typed something into the computer. "Margaret Lawson?"

"Must be." Daniel flashed another grin. "Thank you."

If the orderly was confused about the fact that they didn't know the name of who they were looking for, it didn't matter. They were already down the hall, retracing Luci's steps. As they strolled down the monotonous hallways, Luci wracked her brain, trying to remember if her grandmother or anyone else had ever mentioned Margaret Lawson. Nothing was ringing a bell the more she pondered the unfamiliar name. So why had the woman known her grandmother? And why was there a photo of the woman with her grandfather?

There was only one person who could answer that, and they were heading toward her room now.

The door was open, and Daniel strolled in without hesitation. Margaret was sleeping, snoring softly. The same nurse who staunchly determined that Luci couldn't visit had her back to Luci.

"Excuse me, Nurse," Luci whispered. "I'm sorry to interrupt. I don't know if you remember me, but—"

The woman turned, and Luci cut herself off, frowning slightly as she was taken aback. It wasn't the same woman, after all. This woman had the same haircut and general build, however, she was much younger, around Luci's age. Luci suddenly felt rather awkward. She realized that the woman was dressed in jeans and a blouse. Not exactly a nurse's clothing.

"Sorry," Luci apologized, color rising to her cheeks. As she attempted to speak, the words stumbled in her mind before reaching her lips, leaving her unable to articulate anything coherent. Mercifully, Daniel stepped in.

"I'm Detective Flinn," he said softly. "This is my friend Luci. Is this Margaret Lawson?"

The woman nodded, her brow furrowed with confusion. "My grandmother. I'm Willow. Can I ask what this is about?"

Daniel held out the photo. "Is this your grandmother?"

Willow took it, blinking wide, green eyes that grew even larger as she took in the photo.

"I'm pretty sure," she answered, handing it back.

"Does it mean anything else to you?" Luci asked. "Do you recognize anyone else?"

Willow shook her head. Luci tried to keep her exasperation in check. She was sure she'd found proof that someone could explain why Fenton knew her Grandparents. The frustration felt like she was beating her head against a stone wall.

"Can I talk to her?" Luci asked hopefully.

"You can try," Willow exhaled with a suspicious tone in her voice. "I don't think it's going to do you any good. She hasn't been herself lately."

Even through the suspicion, there was a trace of sadness in her eyes and tautness in her features. Her face looked a little pale and drawn as she regarded the two newcomers. She didn't look as though she had gotten much sleep lately.

"I'm sorry to hear that," Daniel said compassionately. He must have picked up on the same subtleties that Luci had because his voice softened significantly as he adopted a more personal tone. "How long has she been in here?"

"A couple of years," Willow replied. "She's gotten worse the last few weeks."

Something about that made her skin prickle. "Do you know exactly when?"

"It's not like I kept track," Willow retorted, more than a little icily. Then she sighed and rubbed her eyes. "Sorry. I'm just exhausted. It happened sometime in the last month when she started deteriorating faster than we anticipated. Truth be told, she was slowly slipping away from us before then. The last few weeks haven't been easy. I'm sorry, why do you have a photo of my grandmother?" Willow asked, seemingly having a moment of clarity as she glanced toward the photo again.

"We're doing some investigations into a body we found recently." Daniel held up the photo again. "We found this photo in the same area. We're just doing some follow-ups."

"I don't know what Grandma Maggie would have to do with it. Though, that is definitely her."

At that moment, Margaret stirred and opened her eyes. She blinked blearily at Daniel and Luci.

"Mrs. Lawson," Luci said softly. "Do you remember me? I was here the other day."

One of Margaret's eyes was clouded by a large cataract. Her wrinkled brow furrowed and she squinted at Luci.

"What?" she asked.

"You called me Annabelle," Luci prompted, hoping that the name would jog her memory.

"Wait, what?" Willow asked sharply, looking from her grandmother to Luci to Daniel.

"Annabelle? Oh my, it is you, isn't it? How is Joseph? I haven't seen either of you since..." Margaret trailed off as if she couldn't remember the last time she had seen Annabelle or Joseph.

"You've been here before?" Willow asked, suspicion blanketing each word, overriding any sign of exhaustion that had leaked into her voice.

"I was visiting someone else and walked by here," Luci explained. "She had called me by my grandmother's name."

Willow looked as though she wanted to ask more questions. Luci couldn't blame her. Instead of leaving an opening for barraging her with the flood of questions that Luci anticipated, Luci turned back to the elderly woman in the bed before her and saw that, despite preparations for an inquisition, Margaret had already drifted back to sleep.

"She's not going to be much help to you," Willow noted. "That's an average conversation for her right now. She's just very confused."

"That's all right," Daniel said, glancing at Luci. "Do you mind if we have a look around?"

"If you don't mind my being in the room," Willow rasped. There was a strange edge to her tone that hinted at an edge of unease. She sat down next to her grandmother without another word and softly stroked the woman's hand.

"Thank you," Daniel nodded.

Luci turned toward the set of drawers. She reached for the first one and suddenly felt very self-conscious about what she was doing. She could feel Willow's eyes on her, burning a hole through her shirt. She glanced over at Daniel, he seemed entirely at ease as he began looking through some of the curios on the rather spartan bookshelf. He met her gaze for a moment and gave her a reassuring smile that put her at ease.

They continued searching as Willow watched them in silence. Once or twice, Luci looked back, expecting to see the other woman on her phone or reading. No such luck. She was staring at her and Daniel every time, as if unwilling to let either of them out of her sight. Luci could understand that. They were going through her grandmother's personal belongings after all.

There was a pile of magazines tucked in a basket next to the Chesterfield. Luci was about to gloss over them when something caught her eye. Something almost imperceptible was tucked between two of the magazines. If she hadn't done a double take, she would've missed it. Based on the way it was peeking out, it didn't seem like a scrap sheet of paper had inadvertently fallen down.

Frowning, Luci bent down and pulled the piece of paper from between the magazines.

Henry Kingston, 78, died Saturday, September 16 of natural causes. He is predeceased by his wife, Angela, and their daughter Rachel.

"What'd you find?" Daniel asked. Stepping behind Luci, he peered over her shoulder, near enough that had she eased half a pace backward she would have felt the warmth of his body against her own.

"Not sure," she replied, trying not to notice how close he was. "It's an obituary from the Denver newspaper from last month."

"Really?" Daniel reached over her and took the paper from her hand. As he did, Luci crouched down and rummaged through the magazines to try and find more of the newspaper. "Ms. Lawson, do you know a Henry Kingston?" he asked, coming up empty.

"No." Willow's voice grew closer, and Luci looked up to see the woman taking the obituary from Daniel. She scanned it, frowning. "No, I've never heard of him."

"Your grandmother never mentioned him?" Daniel prompted.

Willow shook her head, her eyes clouded with confusion as she looked over the paper.

"So you have no idea why she would have this?" Daniel gestured at the paper.

"No, of course not." Willow's eyes were scanning the page over and over again, clearly trying to make sense of it.

Luci, for her part, was trying to remember if her grandparents had ever mentioned the man. His name didn't ring any bells that she could recall. The obituary was sparse on information, which made sense if he had been predeceased by both his wife and his daughter. It was sad to think that there hadn't been anyone to write a more detailed and thoughtful obituary. However, that didn't explain why it was here.

"What's going on here?" A deep, authoritative voice demanded. The other three turned to the door, where a short man with the same light-brown hair color as Willow stood in the doorway, scowling. He looked from Willow to Daniel and Luci. In spite of his small stature, he somehow seemed to look down on Luci.

The man turned to look back at Willow. His eyes moved to the paper in her hand. "What's going on?" he repeated.

"Christian, this is Detective Flinn and Luci," Willow stated about the two strangers. "They're here about a death. Luci, Detective Flinn, this is my brother, Christian."

Christian's eyes narrowed and he stepped forward. "If my sister is under any sort of suspicion, I'm not going to let you bully her," he growled.

"Your sister isn't under suspicion or in any sort of trouble," Daniel promised.

"They're here about Grandma," Willow explained.

If anything, Christian's distrust seemed to deepen. His shoulders stiffened. Luci noticed as he did that his clothes looked worn and frayed around the edges. They still fit well and were well cared for, but it still looked as though he'd owned them for years.

"What on earth would my grandmother have to do with a murder?" he asked. "She's old and confused. I can't exactly imagine her getting out of bed and murdering someone, can you?"

Daniel raised his eyebrow. "Did I say murder?" he asked conversationally.

"Of course, it's about a murder or suspicious death," Christian scoffed. "The police wouldn't be involved otherwise."

"Christian…" Willow started, a bit of a pleading tone in her voice. "They're just trying to get some answers."

Christian folded his arms, locking eyes with Daniel and giving him a steely gaze. "I have no idea what my grandmother would have to do with any of it."

"Mr. Lawson," Daniel began. Lawson held up a hand halting him, still unsmiling.

"I'm going to have to ask you to leave, Detective." He hissed the last word like it was poison. "Thank you for coming; however, unless you're arresting someone or have a warrant, I believe my grandmother needs rest."

Luci glanced at Daniel, assuming he would argue or push for more information. Instead, he nodded, though it seemed he was reluctant.

"Thank you for your time, Ms. Lawson." Daniel pulled his wallet from his back pocket and fished around in it until he pulled out a card and handed it to the woman. "Please don't hesitate to contact me if you recall anything, no matter how insignificant it may seem."

"Not likely," Christian muttered under his breath.

Chapter 12

Chapter Twelve

"Are you okay?" Daniel looked over at Luci as they made their way back through the halls of the nursing home toward the exit.

"Just frustrated," Luci sighed, her brow furrowed in annoyance. Typically, she only reached such levels of irritation in the early mornings, before her two cups of coffee had a chance to take effect. This case felt like an endless carousel - circling the same unsolved questions without answers in sight. This nagging ambiguity naturally frustrated Luci. Moreover, there seemed no useful channel for this irritation; every attempt only led to more roadblocks hampering her search for answers.

"I understand." Daniel patted her on the shoulder comfortingly. "I've been there before on several cases when you feel like there aren't any other options and people are stonewalling you whenever there's a chance you can actually get answers. It's the worst."

"I'm glad I'm not alone," she acknowledged, and genuinely meant it. Finding a kindred spirit just as baffled over the endless twists and turns of the case brought an odd sense of relief. No matter how many promising leads fizzled into yet more question marks, at least they could vent about it to one another.

"You want lunch?" Daniel asked as they stepped back out into the daylight.

Luci's stomach rumbled as she realized how famished she was. "I'm starving."

"Any ideas as to where?"

"There's a soup and sandwich place not too far down the road."

He raised his eyebrows. "Sounds good. My treat."

"I'll never say no when a man offers to pay for my food."

Less than ten minutes later, the two of them were sitting in a small deli, the aroma of fresh bread and grilled paninis lingering in the air. The restaurant was packed, with a string of people that stretched all the way to the door.

It felt strange, sitting across from Daniel at a restaurant. Something about the situation made heat creep up her neck and toward her cheeks. It shouldn't have. They were just two people working on a case together when it just so happened to become lunchtime. There was no reason for her to feel self-conscious. Daniel, for his part, looked entirely at ease.

"So, what did you think?" Daniel asked as they sat. The pleasant din of the room around them was loud enough to have a private conversation, but not so loud that they couldn't hear one another. They were tucked in a corner, and anyone who looked in their direction probably would have assumed they were on a date.

"I think going there raised just as many questions as it answered." She ran her fingers irritably through her hair. "I just want some answers, you know?"

"I get it, trust me. Part of being a detective."

"It would be so much easier if killers would just be considerate and say, 'Oh hey, I did this.'"

"Don't think that works if it's been forty years since the murder," Daniel mused.

"That's the other thing. What if the killer is dead? What if all of this is pointless?" *What if it was my grandfather?* She thought to herself. Based on the expression on Daniel's face, he could already tell what she was thinking.

"It's never pointless," Daniel assured her. "Even if we find out the killer's been dead for years, it's something we have to find out."

"I don't know if I want to know anymore," Luci muttered. She hadn't realized she'd said it until she saw Daniel giving her a quizzical look. "Um, forget I said that."

Their food arrived, the harried waiter setting down a Rueben for Daniel and a turkey and brie for Luci.

"You're worried your grandparents have something to do with it, aren't you?" he asked.

"I don't know." Luci picked up a fry and began twirling it in her fingers as she tried to think of how to explain it. "It's just...I always thought I knew my grandparents, you know? Or at least that I knew my grandmother. But what if I was wrong? The more I look into this, the more I'm starting to think that maybe you're right; maybe there was something more going on that I don't want to see."

He nodded, and his face was refreshingly sympathetic. "I have a cousin that I haven't spoken to in years. We used to be close. Then, when I got older, I realized he wasn't the person I thought he was."

"What happened?"

"He stole from his parents for years. When it finally came out, I didn't want to believe it. I thought I knew him. It's hard when people turn out not to be who you thought they were." There was a pause before he continued. "That doesn't mean your grandparents did anything wrong, Luci."

Luci frowned. "I thought you assumed my grandparents were guilty."

"I don't know," he admitted. "That's what I'm trying to find out. Lucky for me, I also know you. It's hard to imagine someone you're related to being anything other than a good person. I understand that."

Luci raised an eyebrow, tilting her head. "Didn't you just say that your cousin was a criminal? Seems to contradict your argument." Inside she was trying hard not to blush.

"I must be the exception that proves the rule."

"Well, you seemed to have turned out all right, regardless of your nefarious ties to the seedy criminal underworld." Luci waggled her fingers jokingly, making her tone sound a little spooky on the last three words. Daniel, who had taken a bite of his sandwich, smirked with a full mouth, which somehow gave him the appearance of a red-headed chipmunk, made Luci laugh. Daniel, picking up on how he must look, swallowed hard and started laughing. It was amazing how their teasing felt like they'd known each other for years.

"Point is," Daniel continued, once the laughter had finally died down, and the tears wiped away. "I don't think you should dismiss the grandmother you remember because of all this. She was still the person who helped raise you and loved you."

Luci paused. She suddenly felt a pit growing in her stomach and it had nothing to do with the brie. What Daniel had just said made her uncomfortable. For a brief moment, Luci had forgotten about the potential involvement of her grandparents in Fenton's death. For a moment, she felt herself *enjoying* Daniel's company just as...Daniel. She didn't want to think about her grandparents right then. It only invited a swell of sadness. As she lingered over hazy memories, more self-doubt crept in. She started second-guessing some key details that she felt sure of earlier. It was the same thought process that constantly spiraled and was getting her nowhere, and she simply didn't want to think about it anymore.

"Is that why you became a cop?" she asked, diverting the conversation away from her grandparents. "Because of your cousin?"

Daniel snorted before taking a bite of his sandwich. "No, not at all. In all honesty, I probably wouldn't have considered it as a profession if it weren't for the fact that my dad sort of strong-armed me into it. He was chief of police before he retired. I think he wanted his only son to follow in his footsteps."

"He forced you into it? That doesn't seem particularly fair."

His eyebrows raised. "Do you think your grandmother forced you into taking over the library?"

"No. She encouraged it, but it was always my decision. I wanted the library."

He nodded. "There you go, same with me."

"Do you ever regret it?"

He frowned, tilting his head as he considered it. "I mean, there was a time when I really wanted to be a musician."

"Really? Why didn't you?"

He glanced from side to side, then leaned over the table, motioning for her to do the same. She met him halfway, wondering what on earth he was going to say that he wanted to keep this secret.

Their faces were inches apart when he moved his lips closer to her ear. His warm breath caressed her skin, sending shivers through her body that she hoped he didn't notice.

"I'm tone deaf and never learned to play an instrument," he whispered, then gave a wide, mischievous grin.

"Jerk," she said, laughing as she sat back in her chair. Daniel shrugged nonchalantly, looking incredibly pleased with himself.

"It got you laughing, at least," he remarked. "I don't like seeing my friends unhappy."

"Friends?" For some reason, the casual way he threw out the word as if he'd said it a dozen times, took her by surprise.

"Well, I'm not sure what else to call you," Daniel pointed out. He put down his sandwich, interlacing his fingers and resting his chin on them as he studied her. "You're not a partner, because you're not a detective. You're definitely not just the librarian who found a body at work anymore, either. I happen to like you and get along with you, so you're certainly not in enemy territory. 'Friend' seems like the best word." He raised his eyebrows. "Unless you've secretly been behind the killings the whole time. In which case, I'm pretty sure you would have to be my personal Moriarty, considering how well you've covered your tracks."

"I'm nowhere near smart enough to fall into that category," Luci laughed. The thought of her being anywhere as clever as Sherlock's archnemesis was so inconceivable that she snorted and giggled.

"Then 'friend' it is."

"I think I can live with that."

Chapter 13

Chapter Thirteen

When the library phone rang, Simon fluttered onto the receiver and flapped his wings to get Luci's attention.

'Phone,' he informed Luci.

"If I can hear you say 'phone,' I can hear the ring," Luci said teasingly. As she reached for the receiver, Simon hopped from the phone to her wrist, crawling up her sleeve. She'd long given up on not having tiny talon marks on most of her clothes. "Hello?"

"Hi, I'm looking for Luci Mitchell?"

"This is she."

"Hi! Luci, this is Suzanne, from the public records office."

Luci sat up straight, suddenly alert as a new spark of hope ignited in her chest. "Yes?"

"We have the blueprints ready for you. I'm so sorry it took this long. We've been swamped so it took us a while to process your 21-D and the 18-F. There *was* a slight problem with the 17-A since you were technically supposed to fill out the 17-B, but I managed to take care of that for you, ha ha ha. Anyway, now you just need to come and sign a receipt form to show you received the originals and bring them back, and we're good to go."

Another form? Luci wondered. On second thought, she didn't care. Her pulse raced with excitement to get the blueprints in hand. If they could give her some answers about her grandfather's room, then maybe that could give her a clue about her grandparent's involvement in Fenton's death.

"I can get there later today if that works?" she asked.

"That would be perfect. Especially since I'd need you to fill out a 217-E if you wanted me to hold it for another day, or a 218-E for two to five days."

"No need," Luci said hurriedly. She'd had her fill of public records forms. If she'd needed any more incentive to get the blueprints as quickly as possible, that was it. She grabbed her car keys and purse. "I'm on my way now."

***

Thirty minutes and a form later, Luci was walking back into the library with a thick stack of oversized paper. The blueprints weren't tightly wrapped in tidy scrolls like they were in the movies. Instead, they were in a large packet and clipped together. She itched to jump directly into the pages in that very moment, yet reluctantly restrained herself. The library was still open for another few hours, and she had two more interviewees coming in. She'd rather delve into these when she wouldn't be interrupted.

When she finally turned her attention to the stack of blueprints, after the library closed, she was already frustrated. The first interview had tanked – confirming Luci's initial gut doubts about the candidate's résumé. Desperate at the time, she had hoped to be proven wrong. She wasn't. The man had swaggered in twenty minutes late in sweaty gym clothes, acted like they were on a date, and then—the most egregious sin of all—had started complaining about Simon. She hadn't even asked the second question before she showed him the door.

The next potential had looked promising right from the start. "So Peggi, tell me about how you would approach reshelving returned books if you worked here?" Luci had asked Peggi, a 20-something freshman who had a contagious smile and large round blue eyes that twinkled under her dark bangs. Luci was hopeful the moment she laid eyes on her. She had instantly been drawn to her bubbly presence after the sweaty aftermath of *rude* and *no chance*.

"Oh, I have a wonderful sorting system I'd like to use! To make things really efficient, I would rearrange all the returned books by color and size rather than by genre or author," she had explained in one breath.

"Color and size? That's... intriguing. How exactly would that work?"

"Oh. My. Gosh. It would speed everything up! I'd put all the tallest blue books together, then the next tallest red ones, then the middling height yellows, and so on in rainbow order down to the shortest orange books. Easy as pie!" she had squealed, karate-chopping her hands as she spoke, arranging imaginary books as she giggled her excitement.

"Well, that certainly is...creative, but how would readers ever find what book they need if the order keeps changing based on color and height? The Dewey system allows predictability," Luci explained, her hopefulness tanking faster than online ratings for a bad movie premiere.

"Hmm...I guess I got so caught up in my sorting invention I didn't think about findability. Back to the drawing board, though, maybe my methods can speed things up in your storage rooms if not the public shelves!" Peggi's wide grin had suggested.

Still clinging to the hope of hiring a circulation desk clerk, Luci had asked, "How would you handle overdue notices and fines?"

"Oh, I wouldn't. I think due dates create too much pressure and all materials should be available indefinitely with no consequences."

Lucy had heard enough and had politely guided her out as Peggi continued to reinvent her color wheel of sorting as she was led out of the library. Luci's original instincts rang true once again and she had yet to find another suitable staffer.

Pushing the irritation to the back of her mind to focus on the blueprints, she pulled them out of her office and laid them out on the circulation desk. Her pulse quickened in excitement as she looked forward to seeing the schematics. Not only because she was curious about what information they might tell her about the layout of the basement, but also because it felt like an old piece of history she'd get to unravel. Learning about Juniper's history and the library's origins stirred in Luci a profound connection, drawing her closer to the soul of the town and the grandparents she held dear.

When she flipped open the packet, she found photo-copied tidy, hand-drawn drafts. Comments in easy-to-read block letters ran around the margin while labels identifying various rooms were scribbled across the paper. When she flipped to the next page, she found a much more intricate schematic, showing HVAC and electrical drawings, neither of which she had the faintest clue how to decipher.

She'd never read blueprints before. Part of her had expected the simple plans that she'd initially come across - like she'd seen in movies. Scanning the layouts of the water pipes and electrical wires was somehow even more fascinating, albeit somewhat confusing. If she hadn't been on a mission, she might have curbed her haste and explored those intricate details some more. Nonetheless, even her fascination couldn't restrain the overwhelming need to see what else might be on the blueprints. She flipped the page and found drawings of the second floor.

At first, everything seemed normal. Both the first and second story blueprints had multiple pages, each displaying different aspects of the construction. When she got to the schematics of the basement, she narrowed her eyes and looked closer. Something wasn't right.

There were multiple versions of the basement layout. One showed the basement as a large rectangular room, the way Luci had always seen it until she had unlocked the new room. The next layout exposed an entirely different basement.

The second basement diagram wasn't hand-drawn, which was strange. It appeared to be created by some sort of computer program. It not only revealed the back room that Luci had discovered but there was more to the blueprint. According to the design, several rooms were supposed to have been built in the basement beyond what was currently there.

"What on earth is going on?" Luci asked the empty library. There was no answer; even Simon, who was watching curiously from Luci's shoulder, was oddly silent.

She flipped back and forth between the two versions, trying to wrap her head around what the discovery meant. The first set of basement blueprints didn't include the secondary room where Fenton's body had been, nor any of the other supposed additions. They were only shown on the second set.

"Maybe I missed something?" She suggested to Simon, still baffled by what she was seeing. "I mean, that's one explanation. Maybe I'm not understanding how the blueprints are supposed to look. Either that, or they stopped construction halfway through."

She glanced at the 'printed on' dates of the blueprints, and then realized why the second set of blueprints had been different. They were more modern and had been designed in the early '80s. The others were dated in the mid-'70s. She speculated that the second set had been used with software that either hadn't been available or was too expensive when the earlier layouts were ready for design and printing. This indicated her grandparents had been planning extensive basement renovations - ones encompassing the mystery room along with numerous others. So why had they stopped early?

To make sure her eyes weren't playing tricks on her, she grabbed the most recent basement blueprint and scurried off toward the basement. She was so intent on uncovering the truth about what the blueprints were telling her that she didn't notice Simon swooping down the steps with her until it was too late. So much for keeping him out of the basement.

She snapped on the lights, unfurled the blueprint, and studied it.

She glanced around her and confirmed that she was in the main rectangle on the schematics. Her eyes flicked over to the stairs leading up to the library. Then they scanned the door, located in the upper left corner of the rectangle. That was the one leading to her grandfather's room. Tracing the route with her finger on the blueprint, she moved past the door and into the unfamiliar storage room.

As she stepped inside the room, an unrelenting draft permeated the room, seeping into her bones. She shivered violently. Even if no one had been murdered there, it was hard to imagine that her grandfather would have been able to tolerate the cold for very long.

When she reached the corner next to the work table, she glanced down at the blueprint, and then back up. There should have been a door near where the table was. She looked at the wall again - no door. It had never been built.

Simon fluttered over to a shelf, perching as he cocked his head, staring at the wall, then waddled as he turned to look at Luci.

'*Cold*,' he squawked, ruffling his feathers.

"I know," she shuddered lightly. "I don't have any way to warm it up right now."

Simon shook his head vigorously. '*Cold,*' he insisted.

"All right, all right. We'll go." She looked around again, still clutching the blueprints. She let out a frustrated huff. "We're not going to find anything new here, anyway."

Simon tilted his head as if sensing her annoyance. With a flutter of his wings, he glided through the air and landed on her shoulder. A cold, smooth beak nuzzled against her cheek as his feathers tickled her ear gently.

'*No sad,*' he instructed.

She laughed and stroked his chest with the back of her finger. "I'll do my best."

Frustrated and with more questions than ever, she trudged back up the steps. A headache threatened as Luci struggled to stop obsessing over the perplexing blueprints; if only she knew someone who could help her read them.

Sighing, she gathered and lined up the papers, ready to put them back to store them. They hadn't been much use after all. Though, Luci thought it may be a good idea to ask and see if they would scan and send the pages to her to keep a digital copy handy. Granted, that would probably involve her filling out another twenty forms just to use their photocopier. Luci wasn't sure if the blueprints would eventually give new information or not, still though, a digital copy would be easier to handle. When she wasn't so tired, she might be able to figure something out. And then—

She froze as her eyes landed on something that stopped her thoughts dead. Her mouth opened in shock as she registered what she was looking at.

She hadn't noticed the name in the bottom right corner of the blueprint until she glanced down as she was lining up the edges. The name of the architect - William Fenton.

Even though it was right in front of her, it took her a beat or two for her to recognize what she was seeing. She blinked, gawking at it, perplexed and unmoving.

"There's no way," Luci breathed, eyes wide. "There's absolutely no way."

Forcing her limbs to respond, Luci flipped hastily to the other blueprints, indicating the first and second-floor layouts looking for the name of the architect. It wasn't Fenton but a person she'd never heard of. Frowning, she went through the remaining schematics for the library. What she discovered was that Fenton's name appeared solely on the '80s blueprints—the ones from when renovations occurred.

Eyes fixed, she stared at the name of the murdered man etched on the blueprint - Fenton had designed the very room where he eventually met his end. She knew that what was in front of her was the truth. She had finally found the connection between her grandparents and William Fenton.

He had designed his own tomb.

Chapter 14

Chapter Fourteen

S tunned by the revelation, it took Luci a few minutes to gather her thoughts and make them coherent. Frowning, she went over to the computer and began typing furiously. Simon perched himself on top of the monitor and looked down, watching her type upside down.

"William Fenton + Mitchell Library" gave her nothing. There was no connection. Same with "William Fenton + Joseph Mitchell." She kept trying different variations of words that might link Fenton to the library. The search engines were giving her nothing. Granted, if these blueprints weren't digitized yet, or had only recently been digitized, then that might explain why. Either way, everything about the current situation was impossible to imagine.

Was it impossible, though? After all, he was found here. She knew he must have had some tie to the library, or he wouldn't have been dead in the basement. The fact that he had been doing renovations felt strange to her. If her grandparents had been inclined to do renovations, why wouldn't they have used the initial builder? Why switch? The original builder had done an amazing job. The library has stood the test of time for over fifty years with few structural problems. It was certainly a testament to the soundness of the construction. If the library was only a few years ol: the time they hired Fenton, there didn't seem to be a need to h' different contractor.

And that was another th' *why* had her grandparents wanted to do renovations, and how l' they been able to afford them in the first place? She had seen the 'gers; she knew that the library had been losing money. Why wor' they have done renovations while they were bleeding cash?

He did a lot of pr'ono work.

Sarah's words noed in her head as she mulled over the latest question. That yuld make sense. What if Grandpa Joseph had gone to Fenton beca'se they knew he would be less expensive? Or what if Fenton had cered to do the renovations for free? If her grandparents had wante'to add on to the library, and Fenton was a well-respected architect nd builder who offered to do the work for free or mostly free, th'n perhaps that was why they hired him.

A'other thought struck her as she trotted back into her office, renrning a few minutes later with the stack of old ledgers she'd been poring over earlier. As she opened and spread them out to the side of the blueprints blanketing the circulation desk, she checked the date on the blueprint by Fenton—1981—then found the book for the corresponding year.

1981 had been another year in the red. Except by the end of the year, the numbers had begun to climb in the library's favor. When she pulled up the one for '82, she saw what she remembered the first time she went through the books. The money began pouring in, and the library's fortune suddenly began to change.

That's when things began to look up for the library; a little over half a year before Fenton went missing, Luci thought.

Something had stopped the basement renovations early and at the same time, something had also drastically increased revenue. What had caused such a spike in revenue after Fenton was hired and why did he disappear less than two years thereafter? If she could figure out what had happened, she was certain everything else would fall into place.

The only problem was that all of the people she knew who might be able to answer- Fenton, her grandfather, and her grandmother- were dead.

No, that wasn't necessarily true. Luci snapped her fingers. There *was* someone else that Luci was certain knew something. The crux of the problem was that the person might not remember what *that something* was anymore.

It was time to pay Margaret Lawson another visit.

***

This is starting to become a second home, she thought to herself as she entered the nursing home for the third time in about a week. Part of Luci yearned to call Daniel, yet intuition held her back. This puzzle was hers to solve. The answers would shape her grandparents' legacy, for better or worse. She needed to be the one uncovering any buried truths. If she found out anything, she would call Daniel. If whatever she discovered exonerated or convicted her grandparents, she needed to hear it first.

Granted, based on the way Margaret had been the last time Luci had tried to speak to her, she wasn't sure if Margaret would be in any sort of state to give her any information. Since Sarah did not know of any connection between her brother and the library, Margaret was her last living hope. Luci also questioned why Fenton and her grandparents seemed to have kept their relationship a secret. Margaret may not be able to answer that; Luci just hoped that she would be able to answer *something*.

There was no orderly at the desk when Luci arrived. She waited around for a couple of minutes, then decided to head on to Margaret's room. If someone stopped her, she would simply explain that she was following up on an active investigation. Not exactly a lie...

She followed the halls, the subtle familiarity of the patterns guided her back to Margaret's suite. She might have to twist Willow's arm if it came down to it and it would definitely be a problem if Christian were there. Though psyching herself up through imaginative hostility didn't exactly work. She opted to go with her charm and persistence instead.

The moment Luci rounded the next corner and spotted Margaret's room, she knew something was terribly wrong. Stepping slowly up to the room, she saw an empty, sterile-looking bed. The comforter that had once snuggled warmly around the older woman, from her last visit, was nowhere to be seen. The curios and photos that had covered the Chesterfield and bookshelf were gone, as were the pictures on the wall.

An ominous sense of dread washed over her as she stepped into the room. It looked unlived in, as though it were waiting for a new resident.

She took a step back and double-checked the golden room number. This was Margaret's room. So where was Margaret and all of her things?

"Can I help you?"

Luci spun on her heels to see the woman from the first visit, the nurse. She was regarding Luci with undisguised suspicion.

"Sorry," Luci put on her most disarming smile. "I was looking for Margaret Lawson. Was she moved?"

The woman's face fell. "I'm sorry. I'm afraid she passed away the night before last."

The bottom dropped from Luci's stomach as she saw her carefully crafted plan to get information vanish in the blink of an eye. She felt a whirl of emotion churning inside her belly. She was both sad that a woman had died, and yet frustrated at another source of information drying up. Everyone who could give her answers seemed to be dead. And the few remaining people that had been alive at that time knew absolutely nothing. How was it possible to solve a forty-year-old murder when so few people alive could give you answers?

That despair and feeling of dealing with a Sisyphean task was so disheartening that it was tempting to just give up. What was this going to do anyway?

The woman was still watching Luci with distrust, Luci realized she had been standing still and staring at her for several moments now. She needed to say something or she was going to get kicked out, and then any hope of getting any information whatsoever would fly out the window. She couldn't lose the few threads she had.

"Oh, I'm so sorry," she sympathized, pulling herself out of her downward spiral of frustration and helplessness. Someone had died, after all. Luci felt a ping of guilt tighten her chest as she said, "You were her nurse, weren't you?"

She nodded. "She was one of my favorite patients. Always had a kind word for me, even when she was starting to slip. I need to ask, are you her family?"

"A family friend," Luci hedged. It was as close as she could get without outright lying. "Her family and mine go way back. I'm Luci."

"I see. I'm Erica."

"Did you know her particularly well?"

Erica bobbed her head from side to side as she waggled her hand in a so-so motion. "We're encouraged not to get too close to patients for obvious reasons. It's not always so easy because Margaret was one of my favorite patients. She also loved to chat, so it was impossible not to get to know her, you know?"

Considering Luci had only known about Margaret for approximately a week, she didn't. At all. Luci nodded and smiled wistfully as if reminiscing about Margaret. As she did, a thought struck her. She might be able to get the same information from Erica that she could have from Willow, at least about the last few months.

"I don't suppose she mentioned my grandparents at all? Annabelle and Joseph Mitchell? They were really close when they were younger."

Erica scrunched up her face in concentration, then shook her head. "I don't think so, not to me at least."

"What about a William Fenton?" Another head shake. "Henry Kingston?"

The last name had been a shot in the dark, hopeful that it would spark something. It did. There was a hint of recognition on her face at the mention of his name.

Erica furrowed her brows in concentration for a moment. Luci waited, her breath held, and her body tense. "That one does sound a bit familiar."

A flicker of hope leaped through Luci and her pulse quickened. "Do you remember what she said about him?" she asked hurriedly. It was a gamble since there was still no connection between Fenton and Kingston, however, there had to be a reason Margaret had held on to that obituary.

Erica shook her head. "Hmmm, something about him being dead. I think this means she could do something she couldn't do earlier. She was in and out of it, and that was around the time she started getting really confused. I'm sorry, I don't know if it meant anything."

"Don't be," Luci smiled. "I appreciate your time."

Luci stepped by her and made her way out, frowning in contemplation as her thoughts swirled like a storm in her head.

No matter what the nurse had said, she had to wonder if maybe Margaret's comment about being able to do something was more coherent than Erica thought. After all, she had kept the obituary. That's not something a person would normally do unless it held sentimental value.

What was worse was that she still didn't have any proof Margaret was connected to the library beyond the photo and her calling Luci by the name Annabelle. There was no proof that she had been connected to Fenton's death or any of this mystery.

Now the last person who could have answered that question... was dead.

Chapter 15

Chapter Fifteen

"Do you have any experience in handling manuscripts that require special care?" Luci asked.

She tried to keep her optimism in check, though it was hard. The latest interviewee, Liam, seemed absolutely perfect. He was well-spoken, he knew the Dewey Decimal System, and seemed to understand how best to handle library patrons better than anyone else she had interviewed.

"I worked in the Special Collections section of the university library when I was getting my Masters," he grinned. He seemed entirely at ease, smiling as he relaxed in the chair. He wasn't cocky with his answers, rather he was simply confident in his abilities. His hair was a startling platinum blond that looked more natural than dyed. It contrasted with the smile lines and creases on his forehead and around his eyes that spoke to his age. "Granted, that was close to twenty years ago. A couple of the other libraries I've worked at had similar collections, so naturally, I had to know how to work with those manuscripts - even if I was in other departments."

Simon flew over and landed on Liam's hair. The parrot tilted his head, looking down at his new roost.

"What do you think, Simon?" Luci asked. Liam, for his part, didn't seem alarmed or concerned that she was asking a parrot for his opinion or the fact that there was a parrot on his head.

Simon considered Liam for a long moment, shifting from foot to foot, his talons picking up pieces of hair. Liam had a small smile on his face.

"That tickles," he laughed.

'Food?' Simon squawked.

"Probably nothing that you can eat," Liam arched an eyebrow, looking questioningly at Luci.

"Finally someone who doesn't immediately listen to him and asks me first," Luci joked.

Simon gave her what could've only been a parrot's glare and ruffled his feathers irritably.

'I am Overlord,' he responded. *'Not good. No food.'*

Luci closed her eyes in exasperation. "Him not giving you food doesn't mean he's a bad choice," she pointed out.

'Not good,' Simon argued.

Luci gave the parrot a frustrated glare, then sighed, turning to Liam. "Sorry about that," she voiced. "Sometimes he can be a bit on the stubborn side."

"It's all good," Liam told her, still looking upward at his hairline as Simon continued to perch on his head. "If I'd known he was here, I definitely would have brought some food to bribe him with."

"Right." Luci rummaged through the papers on her desk as she searched for the résumé she had just set down a moment earlier. "I think that's everything on my end. I've got a couple of other interviews that I need to take care of, though I must say that this went pretty well. I think you can expect to hear from me in the next week or so if I want to move forward."

That was a lie.

There were no more interviews. She was certain she'd found the perfect man for the job, and she was ecstatic. Previous hires and fires had taught her that she also knew better than to offer the job on the spot. She wanted that initial excitement to die down to make sure she was making a smart, rational decision, rather than acting out of relief because she'd finally found a fully qualified candidate.

"Great." He beamed and pushed himself out of the chair. Simon fluttered off his head and landed on Luci's shoulder. He nipped gently at her ear, and she couldn't tell if it was out of affection or annoyance on his part. "I hope to hear from you, then."

Luci led him out of her office and into the main library through the breakroom. As Patrick emerged behind the reception desk, he straightened to attention, trying and failing to hide the open book from his boss' view.

"Thanks for coming, Liam," she called out as he walked around the desk and headed toward the front doors. "Have a great day."

Patrick waited for him to leave the building before turning to look at her. "I'm guessing the interview went well for once?" he asked. "I've never seen you look this excited after an interview. You look like you're on cloud nine right now."

"He has some good qualities, yes," Luci agreed, still trying to keep her optimism in check. "I don't think it's a bad idea to see how he does."

"You're not going to hear any complaints from me," Patrick promised. "It'll be nice having an extra set of hands."

"No kidding," Luci sighed, running her fingers through her hair. "It's getting to the point where I can't do this anymore."

"Well, for what it's worth, I think you've been doing a great job, all things considered. Not many people could handle the library the way you have, especially not with all the other stuff going on. I'm surprised you didn't throw your hands up and storm out the instant a second body showed up."

"It's my home. Though that does raise an interesting point—why didn't you?"

Patrick tilted his head, considering for a long moment. Then, he shrugged. "I like it here, I guess. And I can't imagine many other bosses would let me read on the job."

"Only when it's slow," Luci reminded him. "I've got more complaints about your punctuality if we're going to go down that route, mister."

Simon squawked excitedly and soared over Luci's head to where Nick and Petra were walking through the door. Nick, to Luci's exasperation, already had an apple slice in hand and was handing it over to the self-proclaimed Library Overlord. Simon happily ate his offering while resting on Nick's head as he and Petra walked toward The Bookists' meeting room. The two of them waved at Luci and Patrick as Simon launched off Nick's head and came back to Luci.

'Got food,' Simon said, clearly proud of himself.

"I saw," Luci responded, running a knuckle along the bird's chest. "Don't expect the same treatment from me."

'I am Overlord.'

Simon soared off before Luci could contradict him, his go-to method for winning an argument.

Over the next few minutes, the rest of the Bookists trickled in for their meeting, all greeting Luci with a friendly wave before heading to their room. As she watched intently, a realization struck Luci so glaringly obvious that she berated herself for overlooking it before then. Some of the Bookists were in their 60s. Roger was 70, Luci knew, and he'd lived here his entire life. They would have been alive when

Fenton went missing, even if they'd only been in their late teens to early twenties. She'd kept the crime under close wraps as Daniel had asked but if there was a chance one of the older Bookists members could give her some of the answers she'd been missing, she had to ask.

Excitedly, she swiftly glanced at Patrick, who gave her a puzzled look. Without a word, she started power-walking toward the meeting room, holding up one finger behind her as if to say, *hold that thought*. Simon flew overhead, perching on her shoulder as she halted a moment to not bust through the door.

The Bookists had moved the main table into one corner and had formed their chairs into a circle in the middle of the room. She'd given up on asking them not to do that. They were usually considerate enough to put the furniture back when they had finished their meeting, so Luci didn't see a need to chastise them.

She'd given up guessing how many people were members of the Bookists. It tended to fluctuate based on schedule, with people popping in and out as their schedule allowed. Right now, it was comprised of six people: Nick and Petra, Vance, Elaine, Christine, and Roger. They all fell silent when she entered unexpectedly.

Simon fluttered off Luci's shoulder and perched on Nick's knee. He looked up at the human, head cocked.

"Sorry, bud, I finished off the rest of the apple." Nick patted the parrot. "Didn't realize I would get a second visit from the Overlord."

'Food?' Simon insisted. When Nick held up his hands to indicate there wasn't any delectable treat for Simon to enjoy, he ruffled his feathers, clearly disgruntled, and then flew out of the room.

"He's a picky one, isn't he?" Vance noticed.

"I'd say 'fickle' is a better word to describe him," Luci mused. "I'm terribly sorry to disturb your meeting. I have a quick question to ask."

"Sorry, Luci, were we being too loud?" Nick asked.

"We all really liked the book," Petra declared, holding up a copy of *The Martian*. "Sometimes we get a little overzealous when something big happens in the story."

"And hoo-boy, this one was a doozy," Roger whooped. He was reclining in his chair, the book resting in his lap as he smiled up at Luci. "Can't tell you how stressed out I was for that guy through most of the book."

"No no, you guys are fine. Roger, I was hoping that you could help me," Luci wondered. "I have a few questions about the town that I think you might be able to help me with."

"Ah, how lovely it is to be found useful in my old age," Roger sighed dramatically. "I'll remember this for the rest of my few days."

"Drama king." Elaine rolled her eyes with a curled lip, void of any malice in her tone. "I don't know how your wife stands it."

"Are you kidding? She adores everything about me. Anyway, fire away, Luci." Roger gave a goofy flourish with his hands as he spoke.

"I was doing some research into the town," she told him, making up the lie on the spot. "And I came across a missing person's case. I was wondering if any of you have ever heard of William Fenton?"

"Fenton, eh?" Roger rubbed his chin as he considered. "I remember him going missing. It was big news, mostly because it was the only remotely interesting thing that happened in Juniper that summer. No one ever found out what happened to him."

"I remember hearing he got in with the wrong sort and got himself killed," Elaine chimed in. "Granted, I was only fifteen when that happened. I was more interested in boys than news reports about missing men."

"This wouldn't have anything to do with the body in the basement, would it?" asked Petra shrewdly.

"No, of course not." Luci hoped her poker face was good enough. "Just doing some research into Juniper's history. This leads me to my next question, I wonder if you remembered another person. He died recently, Henry Kingston; maybe you'd heard of him?"

The smile on Roger's face evaporated at the sound of the name. "Yeah, I remember him," he responded. "He wasn't exactly a nice person."

"Really?" Luci asked.

Roger nodded. "He was a miner. Both me and Dad worked with him at one point or another. He had a nasty temper on him. Mean sort. Honestly, he was a nightmare to be around."

That hadn't been what she was expecting. If he had been such a terrible person, why would Margaret Lawson have held onto the obituary?

Maybe she was in love with him despite it all? She thought. That would explain why she had hidden the clipping. However, something about that didn't seem quite right.

"He was fired at one point," Roger continued. "Got into a fight with another worker. He wasn't too happy about that. I'm pretty sure he threatened to beat up the supervisor when he told Henry he was getting fired."

"Sounds like a lovely guy," Vance quipped.

"Do you know what happened to him?" Luci asked, her attention still focused on Roger.

"Think at some point he moved. Didn't exactly keep track of his whereabouts. There are some people you want to keep in touch with and others whom you wish you'd never met. Those types you'd just as soon forget." Roger looked pointedly at her, unsmiling, his face uncharacteristically somber in a way that made Luci shudder. "Guess which one he was."

Roger's words echoed through her head as she left the Bookists to their meeting. One thing was for sure: Henry Kingston sounded like bad news. Though Roger hadn't given her enough information to be certain of anything, either. She needed to fill in more holes.

Walking back into her office, she closed the door and booted up her computer. All thoughts of a promising new employee were wiped from her mind as she began her new research endeavor. She typed "Henry Kingston" into the search bar.

To her surprise, her search brought up nearly half a dozen police reports, with everything ranging from drunk and disorderly to assault. He'd been sent to prison once before; other than that, he had never been convicted.

She found an old photo of him from sometime in the late eighties, early-nineties. He reminded her of a quintessential mountain man, with a scraggly beard and broad shoulders. There was a mean glare in his eyes that made Luci's skin crawl as she studied those eyes. He didn't look like a man she wanted to cross. She now understood Roger's disdain for the man.

She continued to browse through the search results, but nothing new caught her eye. When she typed in Margaret Lawson and Henry Kingston, no connections between the two of them showed in the search results. On a whim, she even tried to search Kingston and Fenton's names together. Again, the search was fruitless. She felt stuck yet again.

Sighing, Luci closed her eyes, squeezing them together tightly as she tried to figure out why on earth Margaret Lawson, who had seemingly no connection to Kingston, would have held onto his obituary. She thought back to what Nurse Erica had said when she'd mentioned the name. Margaret had mentioned something about being able to finally do something. What would that have been?

If she'd been in love with Kingston, which, based on what Roger had said and what she'd just researched, didn't seem particularly likely, what would she have had to do that required her to wait until after he died? No, it was seeming less and less likely that she'd been in love with him. She'd kept the obituary for a different reason.

It's too bad she never got the chance to do whatever it was she wanted to do, Luci thought. *She died so soon after.*

Her eyes widened and she sat up straight. Maybe she *had* done whatever it was before she died. There was no evidence pointing to the fact that she hadn't. If that were the case, then there was one person who might be able to tell her what it was.

It was time to pay her condolences to Willow Lawson.

Chapter 16

Chapter Sixteen

The day after she asked the Bookists about Kingston, she took her lunch break to go pay Ms. Lawson a visit. It had taken a bit of work to find out that Willow lived on the edge of town, on the opposite side of the ski lodge.

It was a quaint house, albeit a small one. Willow seemed to favor the simplistic lifestyle. The yard was small and tidy, and the house was well-maintained with minimal trimmings and flower beds that were ready for a winter's nap. An old car sat in the compact driveway, which hopefully meant someone was home. Luci clambered out of her sedan and moseyed on up to the front door with a disposable tin foil pan in her hands.

Her hopes of having a quiet chat with Willow instantly dissipated when Christian opened the door. At first, he simply looked confused at the strange woman standing on the doorstep. Then recognition dawned and his eyes narrowed.

"Can I help you?" he asked, his voice icy and distrustful.

"I wanted to extend my condolences," Luci expressed, gesturing down at the pan. "I'm sorry, I thought this was Willow's house."

"It is."

Luci glanced over at the single car in the driveway, then back at Christian, eyebrows raised in silent question.

He sighed. "Willow doesn't have a car. That's mine."

"I see. Is there any way I could talk to her?"

"I don't think so." He reached out to take the pan. "Thank you for the food, though. I wouldn't want to keep you."

Luci didn't hand over the pan. The two stared at one another, neither breaking. There was a long, tense moment, as they both stood resolute. She waited for him to tell her she needed to leave. What she would say if he did? She didn't drive across town to leave without the answers she craved.

"I really need to talk to Willow," she insisted.

"She's not here. If you're only here to talk to her, then I suggest you take your fake offering and lea—"

"Christian," Willow's voice cut her brother off mid-sentence. The young woman appeared at the side of the door, peering around her brother to see who it was. "Oh. It's you, um—"

"Luci," she smiled.

"Right. I'm sorry. Hi, Luci."

"I was just telling her she could leave," Christian said stiffly.

"I was hoping I could talk to you, Willow," Luci volleyed, ignoring the man currently trying to shield his sister from her.

"Christian, stop it," Willow snapped. "You can't police everyone who comes to my door."

Her brother grumbled, shot Luci a death glare, then turned and stalked back into the house.

Willow glared after her brother, then gave Luci an apologetic look.

"I'm sorry about that," she sighed. "He's just taking Grandma's death a bit hard."

"I heard she'd died. I'm sorry for your loss."

Willow took a deep breath and nodded, sadness filling her gaze. Then it turned to confusion. "Wait, how did you know she passed?"

She tried to tell the truth while making it sound as innocuous as possible. "I came to talk to her a couple of days ago. The nurse told me and I wanted to pay my respects." She held up the disposable tin. "I'm a baking enthusiast, so I made you a French toast casserole with homemade brioche."

Willow's eyes widened in surprise. "That's...a lot of work," she sputtered, eyeing the covered dish.

"It was nothing." Luci hesitated, trying to figure out exactly how to phrase what she wanted to say next, and realizing that being straightforward was the only way to go. "I was hoping I could talk to you, Willow. Would it be alright if I came in?"

"Does this have something to do with the death that the officer was asking about?" Willow asked. When Luci nodded, Willow sighed. She looked exhausted, and Luci finally noticed the signs of grief that she hadn't seen earlier: sunken eyes and waxy skin. Her eyes were red and puffy from crying and she looked as though she hadn't slept in a while.

"It does," she acknowledged, although not without some reluctance. "I'm sorry. I shouldn't be asking at all, especially not now. I have to admit though, it's a time-sensitive thing, and I could really use your help. I promise I won't take too much of your time."

"I..." she trailed off, then nodded. "Alright. Why don't you come sit down?"

She led Luci to the living room in silence. They maneuvered through the cramped space, stepping over boxes and nearly stumbling over a cat who gave the two of them an affronted look while refusing to move from her spot in the middle of the floor. The small living room was cluttered with old papers and decades-old knickknacks. The frayed couch sank beneath Luci's weight, the seams looking as though they might split at any moment.

Willow sat opposite her in an old chair, the edges distressed with age and use. There was a brief pause between the two of them. Willow looked at Luci with a peculiar mixture of curiosity and suspicion as she waited to find out just why her visitor was there. Luci, for her part, was straining to hear Christian, since the rest of the home seemed surprisingly silent for there to be a third party in the house.

"So, what is this about?" Willow asked after a long moment had finally passed, bringing Luci's attention back to the task at hand.

"Henry Kingston," Luci began.

Willow sighed, sagging backward in the chair with weariness. "I already told you, I've never heard the name before—"

"I remember," Luci interjected. "I talked to her nurse about him, and she said that your grandmother mentioned something about needing to take care of some unfinished business and it somehow involved him. I was wondering if your grandmother had mentioned anything similar to you, or if she had done anything strange before she died. Maybe in the last month?"

"Her nurse? I hadn't realized they were that close," mused Willow. There was an edge to the words as if something about the situation bothered Willow more than she let on.

"Does anything stick out to you?" Luci prodded, desperately hoping to jog the other woman's memory.

Willow chewed the inside of her lip, picking at a loose thread of her shirt as she contemplated the question. Luci waited, holding her breath, certain that Willow was about to give her the information that would blow this entire case wide open. She was Margaret's grand-daughter, she *had* to know. It had seemed like she was at her grand-mother's bedside most days, she must've heard something.

Willow shook her head, and Luci's stomach plummeted.

"I'm sorry," Willow met her eyes. "My grandmother was starting to deteriorate in the last few weeks. She was saying a lot of nonsense that I didn't understand. I don't remember her saying anything about a Henry Kingston or taking care of unfinished business."

The wind seemed to rush out of Luci's lungs. There went her last hope of any connection to this bizarre mystery.

"Did anything she say in the last couple of months or so come off as strange to you?" she asked.

Willow sighed and seemed to humor Luci by scrunching her features and thinking.

"There was the time when she asked me if I liked the book I borrowed from her," Willow shrugged. "Only I hadn't borrowed a book from her in years. She didn't even have that many in her room at the retirement home. Regardless, I told her I liked it and she was happy. I'm telling you, she's been confused for a while, so whatever she might have said was probably nothing."

That bubble of last hope burst in an unpleasant explosion. She had no idea where to go from here or what sort of information might be useful to her. There was nothing more for her to ask at this point.

"I'm sorry I couldn't be of more help," Willow said. "I don't know what you're looking for, but I hope you find it. Whatever *it* is."

I'm starting to think I never will, Luci thought with a hint of bitterness. That was how this case had gone so far. Everything she'd tried to figure out had either led to a dead end or more questions than she knew what to do with. It was beginning to feel like an infuriating effort in futility, and she wasn't sure what else she could do at the moment to prove her grandparents' innocence.

Luci knew that wasn't Willow's problem. She'd just lost her own grandmother. Her eyes were still red and puffy, and her waxen complexion gave her a peaked look. She didn't need to pester this woman anymore. Luci knew what it was like to lose a grandmother. She plastered on her best smile, hoping that it at least looked slightly genuine because it was despite the despair of the unknown clenching her heart.

"Thank you," she whispered. She stood. "I won't waste any of your time."

"I'm sorry I couldn't be more helpful," Willow stated. "I'm not exactly sure what you're looking for, although, if there's anything else I can do for you, I'm happy to do my best."

There was something stiff and formal about the words that made Luci doubt their veracity. Luci quickly dismissed the thought. She knew there was a chance she was just being cynical and bitter about the lack of answers that had nothing to do with Willow.

"I appreciate it," Luci kicked up the corner of her lips, trying to inject at least a modicum of sincerity into her words. She wasn't sure how effective she was, though. "Thank you for talking with me, and, again, I'm sorry for your loss."

Biting back the sting of dispiritedness, she started heading toward the front door. Just as she was about to leave the tiny living room, her eyes landed on an open cardboard box. She stopped dead in her tracks to the point where Willow ran into her.

"I'm so sorry," Luci said, stumbling forward slightly, with her eyes locked on the box. She couldn't believe it. What she had just seen was impossible. Absolutely absurd.

Hands shaking with excitement, she crouched and looked in the box, making sure that she wasn't seeing phantoms. She wasn't. There they were, plain as day.

"What is it?" Willow asked, puzzled.

"I-I'm sorry. I just..." Luci trailed off. As if in a trance, she hunched over and stared at the old photograph that was sitting on top of a pile of junk. Her hand trembled slightly as she reached for it.

It was a young Margaret, somewhere in her mid-twenties. She was beaming, leaning against a man who had his arm wrapped around her as they stood in front of the Grand Canyon, cast in a golden hue from the sunset behind them. Luci focused on the man. There was a ringing in her ears as she tried to tell herself that she was imagining it. She knew she wasn't.

"Willow," Luci spoke slowly as if speaking too quickly would intimidate the answer away. "Who is this?"

Willow took the photo Luci was holding out, tilting her head to study it.

"I don't know," she muttered. "It was in Grandma's belongings. I don't think I ever knew who the man was."

"Would your brother?" Luci's mouth was dry, her heart racing so quickly that it threatened to beat out of her chest.

"Would I what?" Christian appeared as if by magic—*or as if he were spying on us*, Luci thought.

"Do you know who this is?" Willow showed her brother the photo.

Christian barely looked at it. "I'm pretty certain that was Grandma's first fiancé'," he surmised. "She kept the photo even after she met Granddad. He disappeared or something a long time ago."

Luci's eyes bulged at the words. She glanced down at the happy couple, staring up out of the portrait.

Her intuition had been right. Margaret Lawson had been connected to the body in the library.

She'd been engaged to William Fenton.

William's face beamed at Luci, completely oblivious to the fact that his body would one day be found at her library.

Chapter 17

Chapter Seventeen

L uci's throat ached slightly as she fell silent, finishing a recap of her escapades over the last few days to her increasingly disgruntled, one-man audience.

"So, when were you going to tell me all this?" Daniel asked, his brow furrowed as his lips turned downward in the faintest of frowns. "Because I'm pretty certain this qualifies as things you definitely should have told me the instant you found out about them."

"When I knew it was important," Luci responded. "Which, funnily enough, I happened to figure out about five minutes before calling you."

They were sitting in Luci's office, Daniel leaning forward with his elbows on his knees, his hands clasped in front of him. He sent her a last glare before he leaned back in his seat as he mulled over everything that Luci had just told him. He'd listened with rapt attention as Luci told him what she'd discovered, her trip to the retirement home and then to Willow's, her discovery of the photo. At some point, Simon had flown over from his perch to roost in Daniel's hair, his head bobbing as Luci spoke as if paying just as much attention to the story as Daniel.

"You know there was a time when I thought we were working this case together," he said, leaning forward again, the parrot still contently perched on his head despite the movement.

Luci grimaced. "Sorry," she murmured. "You're right. I probably should have told you. Though, I also didn't want to waste your time."

Daniel snorted. "Trust me, you're never a waste of my time." She thought he would say more. However, when he next opened his mouth, it had nothing to do with her escapades at all. "Why didn't Willow recognize him in the other photo?" Daniel asked. "The one we brought to the retirement home. She said she didn't recognize anyone."

"I asked the exact same question," Luci stated. "Well, nearly the same. Come to find out, Margaret didn't have many photos of him, and she didn't talk about William to her grandchildren. Since Fenton was bundled up in the photo we showed her, it didn't register. Christian heard a few stories, though that was only because he asked. It's a bit weird that she didn't know, and yet not entirely unreasonable."

"It's still a bit strange," Daniel mused. "Why would Margaret never talk about her first fiancé'?"

"Maybe because it was too heartbreaking. Or because she didn't want to hurt her husband's feelings? Either way, it's interesting, isn't it?"

"It's definitely not what I was expecting," Daniel admitted. "You said you never found the link to Kingston, though?"

"No." She was more than a little frustrated about it. "Neither Willow nor Christian had ever heard of him before we found the obituary. The only thing I've gathered is that he was an ill-tempered miner and, besides being a jerk and arrested twice, he lived a fairly uneventful life. He kept to himself."

Daniel nodded, staring speculatively over Luci's head. "When was he last arrested, do you remember?"

Luci pulled up her computer. "1980," she answered. "That's around the same time when he lost his job with the mining company."

Something pinged in Luci's head as if something was screaming at her that this nugget of information was important. She had no idea why it would be. She glanced over at Daniel. The detective's stoic, yet handsome face gave away nothing as he processed the information.

"It feels like everything we've found is just circumstantial," Luci admitted. She leaned forward, elbowing a tower of books out of the way as she rested her arms on the cluttered desk. "I don't know what else to do at this point, Daniel. I'm sorry."

"Well, you've uncovered that there was something strange going on with your grandparents' finances when it came to the library; now that we know there's a connection between Fenton and the woman who called you 'Annabelle,' we can include that as part of the facts of the case." Daniel rubbed his chin. "We also know that Fenton was doing the renovations on the library that were never completed, though we don't know if they stopped because of Fenton's death or for some other reason."

"I've been searching for the earliest connection between my grandparents and Fenton," Luci told him. "Nothing so far. I can't seem to find anything back then."

"They were about the same age, weren't they? Maybe school friends or something similar?"

"Maybe..." Luci muttered. "Then there's Sarah, William's sister, who didn't seem to know anything about my grandparents."

"Does Kris remember all your childhood friends?" Daniel asked.

Luci opened her mouth to say of course, then closed it, turning the question around in her head: did she remember all of Kris' childhood friends? She remembered the friends who came over every other week and pestered her relentlessly while she was trying to study. Truth be told, that was it. She knew Kris had more friends than just those who came by the house regularly.

And that's less than twenty years ago, Luci realized with a strange chill. *What would she remember when it had been nearly sixty?*

Daniel must have seen the expression on her face since he nodded. Simon, miraculously, had still not moved from Daniel's head, appearing as a little feathered hat that moved periodically on his perch.

"I have siblings, too, and I'll bet that if I asked them to name one of my less well-known friends, they wouldn't be able to. I know I wouldn't, if it were reversed."

She gnawed the inside of her cheek raw as she contemplated what he was saying. He was right, of course. The only people who could tell her how close her grandparents were to William were dead now. For all she knew, they could have been moderately close friends at some point, or they had gotten to know people later in life. They had at least been close enough to take photos together.

Simon squawked, bringing Luci back to the present.

"You can bat him off if you want to, you know," she offered, nodding at the parrot still quite happily nesting in Daniel's hair, cleaning his feathers.

"Nah, he's not bothering me at all," Daniel retorted. "I would hate to offend the library Overlord by dislodging him from his throne."

Simon preened, puffing his feathers out proudly as he basked in Daniel's praise. Luci rolled her eyes as she held a ghost of a smile behind her lips, watching the detective stroke the parrot's chest.

Then she bit her lip, the mood dissipating and growing more somber as another thought crossed her mind. She sighed, as she contemplated how to address the next topic. In the end, it was best to just get it out in the open.

"There is one other thing I wanted to talk to you about," she added. She shifted in her chair as she licked her lips.

Daniel raised his eyebrows. "Don't keep me in suspense," he voiced when Luci didn't say anything. "I'm all ears."

"You're going to think I'm crazy," she began.

"You're assuming I don't already." His mouth quirked upward playfully as Luci scrunched her nose at him. "What is it?"

"I've been thinking about Margaret Lawson's death," Luci admitted. "Don't you think it's a little sudden? As in coincidentally sudden?"

Daniel frowned, eyes glazing over in contemplation. "It wasn't something I'd considered," he admitted. "Besides, you said she had been getting worse over the last month or so, right?"

"That's exactly my point. She only started getting really bad around the time that Kingston died."

"I'm still not convinced Kingston has anything to do with any of this," he sighed. "We don't have any evidence to back it up. Just a few theories."

"C'mon, the timing is so weird," Luci huffed. "As soon as I start asking questions and talking to her, even though she's really confused, she dies?"

"Coincidences happen," Daniel started. In response to the annoyed look Luci gave him, he proffered a smile. "Don't hate me for playing Devil's Advocate."

"You're impossible sometimes," Luci muttered, though with no real ill humor. "Still, you know you can't deny that it's fishy."

"You're right."

She opened her mouth to argue when his words registered and she snapped it shut, eyeing him suspiciously.

"Why do you look so surprised?" he asked.

"I figured you would fight me more, if only for the sake of being a contrarian."

"I do love being difficult," Daniel replied. "However, in this case, all I'm saying is that you can't automatically assume that there's something off. Yet, that doesn't mean I shouldn't look into it."

"So how do I convince you to look into it?" she asked.

Daniel stroked his chin like an ancient philosopher might his beard. "Well, I might be able to help you out... for a price." His eyes glinted with that oddly charming mischievousness she'd come to expect from the playful detective.

"I'm afraid I'm all out of firstborns," Luci quipped. "If you're going down the traditional Rumpelstiltskin route."

"Considering I can't turn straw into gold, I don't think I could go down that route even if I wanted to."

"Name your price."

There was a slightly too-long pause as Daniel considered. His green eyes seemed to scrutinize her more than was strictly necessary. Heat began creeping up her neck as Luci tried to keep her face impassive.

"I'll talk to the coroner in exchange for a batch of your scones once they're perfected," he finally expressed.

Luci tilted her head, brow furrowing. "You want me to bribe you with baked goods so that you'll talk to the coroner?"

"I mean, I'd probably talk to the coroner regardless," he admitted, grinning broadly. "But if I can get some of your pastries in the process, it's not like I'm going to say no."

Luci's snort was so loud that it startled Simon off Daniel's head. The parrot shot Luci a disgruntled glare as he fluttered over to one of his roosts on the wall and settled back down.

Daniel chuckled. "Well now that I'm not a living perch anymore, I think I should probably head out." He stood, stretching. "Thanks for bringing me up to speed."

"Thanks for listening to me and not thinking I'm crazy," she retorted. Daniel cracked a grin.

"I never said that." He teased. "I'll see if I can pull a couple of strings with the coroner. I can't make any promises. There's a chance he won't listen, or won't even be able to perform a proper autopsy, either because he's too busy or because the body's been buried already. There's also the fact that he's still mad that I forgot to leave him coffee that one morning. Regardless, I'll at least talk to him. Perhaps he's into pastry bribes too."

Luci exhaled. The tension she hadn't realized she'd been holding in her body ebbed out of her. Daniel trusted her enough to at least take her suggestion seriously. If there was something strange about Margaret's death, then there was a chance it was linked to the woman's dead fiancé.

Luci might finally get some answers on why the man who had been hired to renovate her grandparent's library had wound up dead and locked in the basement instead.

Chapter 18

Chapter Eighteen

"Liam, could you do me a favor and go through the hold requests and pull those from the shelves?" Luci asked as she spotted her new employee out of the corner of her eye. Most of her attention was focused on the computer screen in front of her at the circulation desk. "I can print off the list for you. I figure it's a good way for you to get used to the layout of the library—"

"Already ahead of you," Liam responded. Luci's head spun around as she stared at Liam in confusion. Then her eyes widened as he gestured to the cart in front of him, a dozen books neatly arranged resting on top, white pieces of paper sticking out of each one.

"I saw the hold list earlier and went ahead and took care of it," he smiled. "Hope that's okay. I've organized them by tags to separate the books by who placed a hold on them. It's how we did it at my old library, so, again, hope that's all right."

"It's...uh, yeah, that's fine." It was more than fine. The fact that she hadn't had to train him was one thing. Taking the initiative while he was still so new was something else entirely. Luci was growing more impressed by the day. He'd taken to organizing the circulation desk and break room - something neither Luci nor Patrick had been particularly consistent with. He had never complained about cleaning the restroom, either. Even his crisp shirt and khaki pants were a far cry from the crumpled t-shirts and jeans that Patrick wore. The cleanliness of Liam's outfits sometimes even put Luci to shame.

It was a relief and a weight off of Luci's shoulders. Having an employee that she didn't need to micromanage and who was enjoying his job was a godsend. Patrick agreed that so far Liam had been an amazing addition to the library. She was starting to wonder how she had managed the last few months without him.

"Thanks," she replied. "It helps a lot. It seems like you're settling in pretty well."

"I like to think so," he agreed cheerfully. "I like it here. The work environment is nice and relaxing. A lot different from the last place I worked. It's cozier; warm and inviting."

"I'm glad," she grinned. "What with how crazy it's been the past few years, having you here allows me to finally catch up on everything I've neglected."

"If you need a second set of hands, I'm always happy to help after work," he offered. "I'm hourly, after all. How late do you normally stay?"

"Depends on the day," she told him. "Anywhere between five and nine. Thanks to you," Luci circled her finger at Liam, "I can do my admin work during the day; meaning, I might be able to go home at a decent time."

Liam nodded. He was already putting the hold books on the empty shelves next to the desk. Normally Patrick would keep getting distracted by an interesting-looking book in the pile and would pause for minutes at a time, lazily thumbing through the first few pages.

"Anything else you need at the moment?" Liam asked.

As Luci thought about what else needed to be done, Simon glided over, landing on the circulation desk in front of Liam. He looked up at the newest employee, head tilted.

'Food?' he asked.

"Is he always this persistent?" Liam laughed.

"Please. He's going easy on you."

Simon squawked in annoyance when he realized he wasn't going to get anything to eat and he soared off overhead.

"Cute guy." Liam watched the parrot soar away overhead. "I always wanted a parrot when I was younger. My sister did, too. Our parents, though, not so much."

"I only got Simon because he came with the library," she commented. "It's a blessing and a curse."

"You inherited the library, right?" he asked. When Luci nodded, he added, "I always thought that if I inherited something, I'd go and explore all the secrets and find all the hidden nooks. I'd make it like a scavenger hunt they'd left for me. Granted, I always imagined inheriting a haunted house where the stipulation in the will was that I had to spend one night in it alone. I don't think my speculations on buildings are necessarily accurate, though."

"You'd be surprised," Luci muttered to herself.

Color rose to Liam's face and he looked around. "I, uh, hate to ask," he hesitated. "Patrick and I were talking and he said that you found a dead body here?"

She closed her eyes. Leave it to Patrick to scare off the new guy. "Yeah," she confirmed, hearing every bit of her exhaustion in the single syllable. "It's been a whole thing. The police are keeping it under wraps, so I'd appreciate it if you didn't talk about it."

"Creepy. And yeah, for sure," Liam looked baffled. "I had to ask because Patrick also told me the guy was brutally stabbed and left to die in a closet, or something like that."

Her head whipped around. "What?" she hissed in surprise.

"Yeah, he said it had something to do with a mafia hit. I didn't even realize that the mafia was a thing in Juniper, but—"

"Patrick," she stated sharply as the second man rounded the corner. He jumped, tearing his attention away from the book his nose had been stuffed into as her words yanked him back to reality.

"What?" he asked. "If this is about me forgetting to brew a new thing of coffee, Liam said he'd take care of—"

"Why are you telling the new employee that a guy was stabbed to death by the mafia in our library?" she asked.

"Oh." Patrick at least had the decency to look mildly sheepish for a handful of seconds. When she continued to glower at him, he threw his hands up defensively, his finger still holding his place in the book. "I was just having a bit of fun," he gushed. "I've never gotten to haze a guy before."

"You didn't need to start now," Luci groaned, pinching her nose.

Liam's head bounced back and forth between the two of them, confusion and surprise growing with every bob.

"So I'm guessing the guy's ghost isn't haunting the history section either?" he asked.

Patrick snorted, then tried to look away when Luci shot another exasperated glare in his direction.

"Uh, no, sorry, man," Patrick murmured. "Just having a bit of fun with you."

"Darn," Liam frowned, his shoulders visibly sinking as his face crumpled in disappointment. "I've always wanted to see a ghost."

"Don't worry about that," Luci clipped, still shooting daggers at her other employee. "You might still get the chance before the week's out."

"I'm going to go see if anyone's dropped anything in the overnight deposit box," Patrick muttered, tucking his book under his shoulder and hurrying away.

"I checked that a few minutes ago," Liam called to his retreating back.

"Someone might have put something in already," Patrick retorted, not looking over his shoulder. "Better safe than sorry."

Luci shook her head in exasperation.

"Sorry," she shrugged. "No ghosts here."

"Shame," Liam sighed. "In that case, I should probably get on with putting these books on the hold shelves."

As Liam pushed the trolley over to the stand of beige, metal shelves, she couldn't help to think just how nice it would be if there *were* a ghost. At least that way she might get some answers about the library or about Fenton's death or how her grandparents might have been involved.

At this point, it feels like that might be the only way of getting any answers, she thought to herself as she stared mindlessly at the computer screen in front of her with no idea of what she had been meaning to do. Her thoughts were now full of ghosts, breaking up the library hazing, and skeleton mysteries to focus on the mundane aspects of the library. With her priorities shifted, Luci tried to bring her attention back to the present task at hand, but she found her brain blocked, refusing to move.

Her conversation with Daniel had taken place days earlier. How long would it take for him to get back to her about the coroner? She glanced hopefully at her phone, hoping to see a text from the detective, even though she knew it would be as blank as it had been the last time she had checked it five minutes ago.

Five minutes later, her phone remained as silent as the grave.

Chapter 19

Chapter Nineteen

T he heat rushed against Luci's face as she opened the oven door. The scones were a perfect golden brown, the coarse sugar on top glistening tantalizingly in the light as she pulled the tray out.

Her stomach rumbled as she admired her handiwork. She was sure she had the recipe right this time. Sam had been right when she'd said it was missing something and needed a smidge more sweetness. That wasn't all though. It also needed something to mellow out the tartness, something that might help smooth over the rough edges of the sharp lemon and raspberry flavors. Eventually, she'd settled on white chocolate and it was time to see if she was right.

Instead of going online and pulling up half a dozen recipes that would have worked flawlessly, saving her time and her taste buds, she kept making adjustments to her own recipe. It was the principle of the matter. Half the fun to her was figuring it out on her own. Her own recipe, her own magic, her own moan of satisfaction made in a scone.

She glanced at the clock. Sam and Rachel were coming over later, and Kris would be arriving home shortly. Luci figured she could get another batch of something in the oven if she wanted to. It was hot and ready to bring forth her next delectable melt-in-your-mouth treat. Bread, maybe?

She couldn't recall the last bout of anxiety that drove her to such a baking frenzy, plowing through bags of flour as therapy. Yet the sweet aroma of baked goods with a cozy-warm kitchen was a more wholesome comfort than any other vice she could have indulged in.

She checked her sourdough starter. It was happy and bubbly and smelled deliciously of soured yeast. It was just begging to be used. Well, she couldn't exactly say no to the starter now, could she?

Twenty minutes later, the bread was proofing in a bowl by the oven. The scones were cool to the touch, and she was about to seize one to taste test when the doorbell ding-donged. She scurried to the door, ready to let Sam or Rachel in so they could become her guinea pigs yet again.

When she opened the door, it wasn't either of her girlfriends standing on the front step. Instead, the outdoor light illuminated familiar red hair and a smiling, freckled face beneath it.

"Hey," she smiled.

"Hey yourself. Is this a bad time?" he asked.

"No, I'm just..." She glanced down at her flour-splattered sweatpants and baggy shirt. Fine for Sam and Rachel. Not so much to be greeting a detective. *Why does it matter?* she asked herself. *It's Daniel.* "Baking," she finished lamely.

He raised his eyebrows. "Making my bribe?" he joked.

"Not quite," she breathed. "Still perfecting them. Soon, though. I'm almost there."

"Well, I can at least provide my part of the bargain," Daniel offered. "Is it alright if I come in?"

She stood back, allowing Daniel to step past her and into her home.

"Smells amazing." He gave an overly dramatic sniff that made Luci give an undignified snort. "Please tell me I can at least taste whatever you're baking, because I don't have a pizza on the way this time and I'm starving."

"They were more of a test run," she warned. "I haven't had the chance to see if they qualify as bribe material just yet."

"So does that mean I can get one for free?" He gave a dazzling, manipulative smile that got another embarrassing snort from Luci.

"Do you use that smile on all your friends?" she teased.

"Only when I'm trying to charm them into giving me food."

Luci shook her head and rolled her eyes, even as she couldn't contain the exasperated smile. "You're too much sometimes. You know that?"

"Funnily enough, I've heard that one a few times."

She checked her phone. "Sam and Rachel are going to be here soonish, so you're free to take your pick before they steal the rest of them." Daniel took a step toward the kitchen and paused as she held up a finger. "Nah-ah, only if you tell me what you've found out."

"Deal."

They strolled into the kitchen. Daniel plucked up a scone and bit into it, closing his eyes.

"Thoughts?" she asked, a little nervously.

"I'm starving so it tastes delicious," he replied. At the look she gave him, he added, "It's really good. Is that white chocolate I'm tasting? Did you add too little? Or too much? I can't tell."

Luci took one herself, examined it with a critical eye, then bit into it. She could instantly tell what he meant as soon as the flavors and textures melted over her tongue. The first bite was overwhelmingly heavy on the white chocolate, muting all the other flavors. The second bite had almost none at all.

"It's because I used chunks," she groaned, a little annoyed with herself. "They're not evenly distributed."

"Still delicious, though," Daniel assured her, polishing off the first one and already reaching for a second.

She managed to wait until he was halfway through with the scone before she couldn't wait any longer.

"All right. You got your scone plus one. Don't keep me in suspense anymore. Did you find anything interesting?" She tried not to get her hopes up too high. She was so excited to finally get answers, and at the same time, she knew there was a chance she might not want to hear what he had to say. It was hard not to envision some fantastic revelation that would break this entire case wide open and exonerate her grandparents once and for all. Even as she attempted to keep her expectations in check, she still pictured this all being over soon. It all came down to what Daniel said next.

"After apologizing profusely to the coroner for stealing his coffee and promising to bring him a thermos every morning for a month, he agreed to at least look at the body while it was at the funeral home," he replied. "I explained to him some of her symptoms before she passed, and after looking at her medical record, he said it sounded like someone had been messing with her medication."

Luci's mouth fell open in shock. "I-I was right?" she stuttered.

Daniel raised an eyebrow. "You're surprised?"

"Of course I'm surprised," she blurted matter-of-factly. "I didn't actually think my suggestion was going to lead anywhere."

"We'll see," Daniel hedged. "It's just his initial theory. He said that sudden mental deterioration at that speed can be linked to either withholding medication or giving them something with that side effect. The problem is that the body's been embalmed at this point. The wake was scheduled for tomorrow, and the funeral was the day after.

He's asked to delay it because of the possibility of foul play, and he can still do a toxicology report. He might not find anything, so keep that in mind."

"It's still something," Luci urged. "Frankly, my first suggestion was just a massive shot in the dark. I didn't expect it to go anywhere. What are the next steps?"

"While he's looking into that, there's at least enough probable cause to keep looking into it as if it were a suspicious death. At least until we get evidence that says otherwise. I plan to talk to people at the nursing home. Check and see who had access to her medication and who might have tampered with it. I need to cross-check the staff - the nurses, visitors, and anyone else who had access to her."

"You should probably check Willow and Christian as well," Luci suggested. "I think Willow was there a lot. I don't know about Christian. He definitely didn't like us poking around all that much. He's a sour one, I'm warning you."

Daniel nodded. "Noted. That was already on my list of things to do," he confirmed. "Though I've already gotten a phone call from the brother demanding an explanation as to why they can't bury their grandmother. He isn't particularly happy, so I doubt he's going to like me asking him questions. Sour indeed."

"Good luck," she mouthed, thinking back to how grumpy the brother had seemed the two times she had encountered him. Maybe she was being unfair to him, Luci thought as she guessed, "He's probably just struggling with losing his grandmother."

"That's always possible," Daniel agreed. "Either way, I have to treat him as though that has nothing to do with it until I can come up with something concrete."

His eyes had grown distant, his gaze unfocused as a small frown formed on his full lips that looked unnatural on his normally cheerful and personable features.

"What aren't you telling me?" she asked, startling Daniel from whatever reverie he was having. He opened his mouth just as Luci cut him off. "Don't tell me you're not keeping something back. I'm not a detective, but I can at least read you well enough to know that something's off."

The small frown turned into a wry smile that scrunched together some of his freckles. "Can't get anything past you," he joshed.

"There was a dead body in my library for most of my life and I had no idea until about two weeks ago. There are plenty of things that get past me on a regular basis. You just have a terrible poker face for a detective."

The chuckle didn't quite reach his eyes. "Maybe," he admitted. "I think it's time to admit that there is a strong chance that no matter what we do, we aren't going to solve Fenton's murder. The theories we have are flimsy at best and don't have a lot of backing. I hate to admit it, Luci, but we're running out of leads."

"But Margaret—"

"Even if Margaret's death wasn't an accident, there's no real connection between hers and Fenton's beyond the fact that they were engaged."

"So you're just giving up?" The edge of disappointment that crept into her voice was accidental, even so, she didn't try to soften it.

"No, of course not." Daniel shook his head. "I'm seeing this through. I want you to know that there's a chance the trail is too cold at this point. You've seen how hard it is to get any concrete information."

Luci didn't answer. She knew with a taste of bitterness that he was right. "That just seems so unfair," she grimaced.

"It is," he conceded. "Unfortunately, that happens sometimes and there's nothing we can do. One of my first cases, before I moved to Juniper, was a woman who was murdered in a back alley. We searched for months that turned into years to no avail. We simply had nothing to go on. We didn't even know if it was intentional or a crime of opportunity. In the end, the case went cold despite our best efforts. It still eats at me that a potential killer is still out there, and there's nothing that I can do about it."

Luci nodded, chewing on the inside of her cheek as she considered his words and the weight of unsolved murders he must deal with. She knew he was right. Sometimes there was nothing you could do. The thought made her blood simmer.

"I don't want that to happen," she admitted.

A warm, calloused hand covered her own. Taken aback at the sudden touch, she flicked her eyes up to see Daniel's brilliant green eyes on hers.

"Neither do I," he said softly.

Time seemed suspended in the lengthy lull where words stuck in Luci's throat as the two of them stared at one another. That blush crept up her face again, and she tried to think of something, anything, to say.

The doorbell ding-donged again, causing Luci to jump as she extracted her hand from beneath his, the world crashing back around her. She'd been so engrossed in the conversation that she'd completely forgotten that Sam and Rachel were coming over. The conversation ...and his eyes.

"Guess that's my cue to go," Daniel grunted, standing and stretching.

"Right," Luci muttered, trying not to become doggedly stuck on what had just happened. He was just being sweet. "Thanks for coming over and giving me the news."

"I figured you'd kill me if I waited too long," he quipped. Then, he gave a wry smile. "Unlike some people, I happen to tell people right away when I find out interesting stuff."

"You're not going to let that one go, are you?" asked Luci.

"Not anytime soon."

When Luci opened the door, Sam and Rachel were standing on the front step, looking rather disgruntled.

"It's about time," Rachel grumbled. "I thought you were going to have us waiting out here all ni—" she cut herself off and her eyes grew to the size of saucers as she registered who was standing behind Luci.

"Oh," breathed Sam.

"Do we need to come back?" Rachel asked, eyebrows raised as she looked from Luci to Daniel and back again.

"No," Luci gushed, heat flooding her face. "No. Nothing like that. He just came over to talk about the case a bit."

"I see," Sam drawled, in a tone that said very much the opposite. Luci's two best friends gave her matching *you better give us all the juicy details* looks.

"I've got to get going," Daniel stated, clearly sensing something that was way beyond his abilities as a detective to handle. "Thanks for the scones, Luci. I'll let you know if I find anything."

He nodded politely to Sam and Rachel, who cleared a path for him as they stared, stupefied. It took them a minute to remember they were standing outside on a chilly October night before they turned and hurried inside.

Rachel didn't even wait for Luci to close the door before rounding on her.

"And when were you going to tell us?" she demanded, a knowing, excited glint in her eye.

"Tell you what?" Luci asked innocently.

"Don't play coy with us," Sam jeered.

Luci rolled her eyes. "He was literally just here to give me some information that I asked for," she replied, "You guys are letting your imaginations wander too much."

"And you are a terrible liar," Rachel said, crossing her arms.

"Is she blushing?" Sam asked, leaning forward and studying Luci's face.

"She is!" Rachel squealed.

"You two are impossible," Luci guffawed, willing her face to go back to its normal pale complexion knowing full well that she was still red as a tomato. "If you guys keep this up, I'm not going to give either of you any scones. *Or* the bread that's going to be heading into the oven soon."

"You're no fun," Sam pouted. Her friends mercifully dropped the Luci-Daniel subject at the doorway and shifted to venting about a self-serving coworker deliberately provoking Sam for a promotion, leaving Luci relieved.

For her part, Luci was quieter than usual. Although she did her best to listen and contribute to the conversation, her mind was too fixated on other things. Not Daniel. At least, not exactly. She was locking that train of thought into a cell in her mind and throwing away the key. Rather her mind was drifting off to fears about what he said about Fenton's case going cold.

The growing kernel of fear in her stomach worried that he might be right.

Chapter 20

Chapter Twenty

Despite Luci's friends' claims to the contrary, Luci's mind was on William Fenton and Margaret Lawson the entire evening and well into the next day. What were the odds of an engaged couple both potentially being murdered decades apart? If Fenton was killed in the eighties, why was Margaret spared until now?

Because she was going to do something that someone didn't want her to do, Luci thought as she sat in her office, pointedly avoiding the paperwork she was supposed to be doing. It would've been pointless, anyway. A sea of concerns flooded her mind that wasn't going to allow her to be able to concentrate on budget and payroll.

There was always the chance that their deaths were unrelated and she could be making all of this up in her head. However, something about the timing of Margaret's death, right when Luci was beginning to dredge up old history, made it seem like they were somehow tied together.

It was time to start at the beginning: the note that had started this whole thing. Who had sent it to her? Whoever had mailed her that key must have known that Fenton's body was in her library. They must have known that sending her that key with that note would have started the discovery of the murder.

Who would have sent it?

It all revolved around the library in some form or fashion. Fenton's body, Margaret knowing Annabelle, the blueprints...it was all connected. She was certain of that. Now the question among so many was, how? She was missing some crucial piece that seemed just out of reach. If only she could find the key to it all--.

She bolted upright, inadvertently knocking her coffee cup to the ground, spilling room-temperature coffee all over the floor. She didn't even flinch at the sound of shattering ceramic. It didn't phase her at the moment as the revelation dawned on her.

Margaret Lawson had mentioned unfinished business in the month before she died. What was more, she had called out to Luci as if she were Annabelle and wanted to speak to her about something important.

The thought that Margaret might have been the killer crossed her mind. That could explain the unfinished business if she was feeling repentant. Though, that wouldn't explain why she was killed.

Luci's pulse raced as her mind became a tempest, the thoughts swirling in her head as she let her theory run wild. She stared at the wall, seeing the puzzle come together as things clicked into place in her mind.

What if *Margaret* had sent her the key and the note when she'd been lucid before her seemingly rapid decline? What if she had sent Luci the key, knowing that it would uncover her fiancé's final resting place?

Why wait? Luci wondered. *If she knew what happened to Fenton, then why would she wait?*

Henry Kingston.

If sending the *key* was the unfinished business Margaret had been referencing, then that would suggest it had something to do with Kingston's death. Somehow, Kingston being alive meant that she couldn't send the key. When Margaret saw the obituary piece, she sent the letter to Luci. Assuming her theory was correct; she still wasn't sure how the two were connected.

The gears were slowly turning in her mind's eye, more pieces sliding together, turning and twisting to fit as the picture started to materialize. The more she stacked the clues, the more it all made sense.

Suddenly, the high of finally having a solid theory came crashing down around her as reality sank back in. It was a great hypothesis, but all of this assumed Kingston was somehow involved. There was no indication anywhere that this was true. Luci hadn't found any connection between Kingston and her grandparents, or the library, or even Fenton. Until she did, nothing was holding her theory together. It was as flimsy as a house of cards. The pieces in her mind's eye shattered across the floor, just like her coffee mug.

Doubt began to creep in as she stooped to pick up the fragments of her mug. Her hand froze as a new idea struck like a lightning bolt, pulling her back into the mystery. If Henry Kingston was somehow tied to the body in the basement, then maybe his footprint was somehow here at the library as well. She wasn't sure what, or how her grandparents might have been involved with him. Of course, if the last couple of weeks had taught her anything, it was that there were a lot of things about her grandparents she didn't know.

She had put the photos back in the basement after she had gone through them. Back then, she hadn't even heard of Kingston, let alone known what he looked like. That would be the best place to start looking. She hurriedly picked up the ceramic pieces and dried up any remaining coffee spill, then grabbed her heavy-duty gloves as she hurried back down to the basement.

It was beginning to feel like a second office with as much as Luci was going down there. When she entered the side room and looked around, she had to admit it was a great room for storage. It had been well-built, clearly designed to hold out moisture as much as possible. All in all, it was a nice room. The only problem (besides the fact that a body had been found there) was the cold. She needed to remember to start bringing a jacket if she was going to spend more time down there sorting, filing, cataloging and the like.

What had the room originally been built for? Family storage or something else? Maybe it was supposed to be a new addition to the library when it was all done. Again, she had to wonder why the rest of the basement level hadn't been built. The obvious reason was that Fenton had died and someone knew it and sealed off the room. This room, however, was entirely finished. She would have thought there would be signs of more chambers if the build had stopped because a man was murdered. However, it looked as though they built the room and then simply stopped.

You're reading too much into it, she told herself, almost scoldingly. *Stop editorializing.*

The truth was, there were plenty of questions she wanted answered, but too much time had lapsed. Daniel had been right when he said that this was dangerously close to a cold case. If she couldn't find any concrete connection between Margaret's death and Fenton's 40 years apart, or if Margaret had died of natural causes, then it was likely that Fenton's murder would go cold. Even if she found a connection, it was possible they both would go unsolved.

The thought was enough to gnaw a hole in her chest. Fenton didn't have many living relatives. Instead, he'd inhabited a nameless tomb for forty years while people walked a floor above his body. It seemed unfair that his death should go unsolved.

Even if they did solve it, there was a chance the killer would never be brought to justice. It had been forty years, and most of the people who could have been involved were dead.

She pushed those thoughts out of her mind. They weren't doing her any good, and the more she went down that path, the easier it was going to be to want to give up. She didn't want to give up. She couldn't. Not after everything she'd discovered thus far.

I'm going to figure this out, she thought, a silent promise to herself, her grandparents and Fenton.

The box she had brought up was right where she had left it, tucked away on one of the shelves. Last time she had gone through it without knowing what she was looking for. Now, at least, she had an idea of what she needed to find. Or rather, who she needed to find.

Sharp claws rested on her scalp as a familiar weight landed on her head. She hadn't realized Simon had followed her down here.

"Hey, buddy," she cooed, reaching up and stroking his breast feathers. "Didn't realize you came down here with me."

'Cold,' he complained.

"If I start coming down here more often, I'll do something about it."

The lighting wasn't that good, as Luci glanced up at the dust-covered light bulb. At the same time, she didn't feel like lugging the box all the way upstairs again, only to have to bring it back down once she was finished. Her eyes landed on the wooden craft table in the corner. That would suffice along with her phone's light.

Not wasting any more time, she hauled the box over to the work table, sneezing from the dust, and began rummaging through the items, looking for new clues that might tell her what she was still missing.

As she studied the photos for the second time, that hope building in her chest ebbed away into despondency. From what she could see, there wasn't anything in the photos that could help. There weren't any other images of Fenton or Kingston, anything that could lead to more clues or connections. She went through them again and again, hoping that she had missed something. The more she scrutinized the items in the box, the more she realized she was pulling at strings.

Throwing the handful of photos she'd been holding back into the box in irritation, she brushed her hair from her eyes and turned around to look at all the other items on the shelves that awaited her attention. One of those might have some sort of clue. They could also end up simply being stuff that held no additional answers.

As she was deliberating her next steps, Simon fluttered overhead and landed on the desk next to Luci. He cocked his head as he studied one of the tools that were still strewn about.

'*What that*' he asked.

"They're tools." Luci followed his gaze to see which one he was looking at. "Specifically, that one's a chisel."

Simon's wings fluttered as he considered the thing in front of him. He waddled a little closer to it, head tilting as he glanced over at Luci.

'*Toy?*' he asked.

"Not toy. Tools. They aren't for you." Simon, however, kept staring at the chisel in front of him. A prickling intuition ran through her body as she observed the intent way her parrot was looking at the chisel. "Simon, don't—"

Before she could even finish saying "Don't play with it," Simon had already clutched the chisel in his talons and soared overhead, out of the room and into the rest of the basement.

"Oh, you've got to be kidding." She dropped the photo she'd been holding back into the box and hurried after the adorable, stubborn parrot.

She only caught a flash of red tail feathers soaring through the door up to the library as she trotted across the basement and up the steps. She expected Simon to be soaring proudly overhead, wanting to play chase the same way he had with the photo. Instead, he was sitting on the circulation desk, cleaning his talons as he waited for Luci, the chisel resting next to him.

'Not toy,' Simon informed her.

"Thanks for telling me," she retorted. "You need to stop taking things that don't belong to you."

He looked at her. She hadn't realized parrots could look exasperated.

'I am Overlord,' he said.

Luci shook her head in fond amusement, reaching for the chisel. When she picked it up, she nearly dropped it out of shock. With trembling hands, she steadied her grip and held it closer to the light, making sure that she was seeing what she thought she saw.

She picked away some of the caked on dirt and sucked in a breath, still processing it all as she held the chisel up to the light.

The dim light in the basement had obscured the details of the tool's handle. Now, with the brightness of the library's overhead lighting, she saw what had eluded her down below.

There was a faint engraving on the handle.

She read and reread the two-letter engraving, trying to tell her brain that what she was seeing was true. She knew that, despite the odds, her eyes weren't playing tricks on her. There was an engraving, and the initials carved into the decades-old wood weren't her grandfather's.

HK

Henry Kingston.

Chapter 21

Chapter Twenty-One

T he room was spinning around her. Henry Kingston had been here. More than that, he had been in the room where they had found a dead body.

You don't know that an infuriating, nagging voice said in her head. *HK doesn't necessarily mean Henry Kingston.*

Who else could it possibly be, though? She ignored the cynical part of her that was saying she needed more evidence. If there was a chance Henry Kingston had something to do with Margaret's unfinished business, and Fenton was Margaret's first love, then what were the odds that a different person with the same initials as him would have left his tools in the same room where Fenton was murdered?

It was too much of a coincidence.

And if one of his tools was there...

Intuition struck and she dropped the chisel back onto the circulation desk, completely ignoring the bemused patron standing in front of her probably wondering what on earth she was doing, and hurried off.

"Someone will be right with you," she called awkwardly over her shoulder, not waiting to see if the library guest responded. She couldn't wait. She had to check the other tools to see if her theory was correct.

Running back to the basement, she grabbed all the tools on the work table she could find, scooping them up in her arms, smearing dirt across her crisp blouse as she cradled them while dashing back up the steps to where the light was better.

She found the nearest empty table and spread the tools out in front of her. The resulting clatter, ear-shattering in the silence of the library, caused a few people to look over at her. She smiled sheepishly, and silently apologized. A couple of the patrons grumbled about librarian hypocrisy, while most simply returned to their work.

One by one, she held the tools up to the light. She scratched at the dirt covering the handle, adding to the clumps that had already flaked off and landed on the once pristine table. She could worry about that later, though. There were more important things to focus on.

After the third one, she felt a grim sense of satisfaction. She'd been right. Exactly one set of the tools had faint yet visible HKs carved into them. The others were unmarked. At least she knew now why there had been two sets of tools. One set had likely been her grandfather's, the other Kingston's. Now the question was, what on earth had Kingston's tools been doing there, anyway? Her grandfather wasn't borrowing them. He had his own. Had Fenton been borrowing them?

What were they doing that required two sets of identical tools? She had forgotten to bring up the tool bag with the second set; however, from what she remembered, they had also looked well-used. If she had to guess, that would mean they were working on the projects simultaneously and needed more than one set of tools. What that project might have been, she had no idea.

She groaned and rubbed her temples. In her mind, this proved almost without a sliver of doubt that Kingston was involved in all of this, which lent credence to the idea that Margaret had sent her the key after Kingston's death. There was something she was still missing that nagged at her. What she had found was arguably an incredible piece of evidence that could give a new lease on life to Fenton's increasingly cold case. Or it could all be a coincidence. She was missing the evidence that would definitively prove it one way or another.

Whoever was involved in this, they covered their tracks well, Luci thought. Had her grandparents helped with the cover-up? There was no link between her grandparents and Kingston, beyond the tools in the library, and the only evidence of a connection between them and Fenton had been locked in a room with his body.

They had to have been, Luci thought with a horrible sinking sensation. *It's their library. Whatever happened here, they helped obscure the tracks.*

It still didn't answer why Margaret had been the one to have the key. Why hadn't her grandfather or grandmother held onto it if they were involved?

"Whatcha looking at?"

Luci jumped, startled out of her thoughts. Glancing up, she saw Liam looking down at her, a kind yet stupefied smile on his face.

"Oh, um..." She glanced at the peculiar spread on the table, the words sticking in her throat.

"You okay?" Liam asked.

"Yeah, sorry," Luci muttered. "Just distracted."

"I can see that." Liam crouched and looked at the tools strewn in front of her. "Anything interesting?"

"Oh, just some old tools that were in the basement," she replied. Explaining the whole story to Liam was going to take way too much time, and she needed to tell Daniel everything she'd just learned.

"Fun." He glanced at them without much interest, then turned back to Luci, eyes sparkling. "I was wondering if it would be possible for me to stay late sometime? Patrick was telling me about how some of the guests were talking about hearing spooky noises over in the biography section, and I was hoping that maybe I could hold a séance or stick around and see if I saw anything."

Luci forced herself not to groan and instead squeezed her eyes shut in frustration. Patrick pulling on the new guy's leg and exploiting his gullibility was the last thing she needed right now.

"Patrick's just having a bit of fun with you right now. There aren't any ghosts or spooky voices anywhere in the library."

Liam's face fell. "Are you sure?" he asked. When Luci nodded, he continued, "Maybe I could stay late one night anyway? Just to see if there is something? A building like this has to have at least one or two ghosts."

"I didn't realize you believed in ghosts in the first place."

He shrugged. "It's not something I usually mention during interviews. Some people get put off by that sort of thing." He suddenly looked nervous. "You aren't, are you?"

"No, not really." She sighed, her mind already composing her text to Daniel as she tried to extract herself from the conversation. "Either way, I'm sorry. You're too new for me to let you stay in the library after hours unless I'm around."

Liam considered this. "That's fine," he mused. "I don't think the spirits would object to having another person there."

"That's not what I..." She trailed off, already recognizing it as a lost cause. "I'll think about it."

He brightened. "That's all I can ask for! Thanks!"

"No promises," she muttered. She wasn't sure if he heard her, and she wasn't sure if it mattered. She'd have to have another word with Patrick about not messing with Liam. Later. What she had just discovered, seemed rather important compared to everything else that was going on - a revelation that she was still trying to come to terms with.

Reflexively, she pulled her phone out of her pocket. Daniel had wanted her to tell him when anything monumental or important happened.

This was monumentally important.

Chapter 22

Chapter Twenty-Two

"I've got something to show you," Luci blurted while at the same time Daniel said, "Have I got news for you."

"What?" they both said with identical tones of bewilderment.

Luci pulled the phone away from her ear, looked at it as though it would provide her some answers, then put it back to her ear.

"You first," she and Daniel said, once again in perfect unison.

"Jinx," they said.

"Okay this is just getting ridiculous," Luci chuckled, finally breaking the spell.

"Definitely one of the weirder starts to a phone conversation," Daniel agreed. "What's up?"

"I've found something," she said, a little breathlessly as she paced back and forth in her cramped office. "Only, I think it's easier if I show you. Can you come by the library?"

"I was actually going to say the same thing. No really," he protested at Luci's disbelieving snort. "Well, I was going to ask if you could come by the police station instead of me going to the library. So, besides that, the same thing."

She looked down at the tools strewn across the table.

"There's kind of a lot of them," she voiced. "Are you sure you can't just come here?"

"Unfortunately, I'm a bit swamped at the moment," he sighed. "I'm drowning in paperwork, otherwise I would be in the car already. Any chance you can bring your mysterious things here instead?"

"I can bring a couple of them, I think." Her eyes darted around until they landed on a cardboard box. "Or all of them, I guess. I think one will get the point across, though."

"I'm intrigued. When can you get here?"

"Can I run red lights?"

"You don't have a police car and you aren't a cop. So, no."

"Give me fifteen or twenty, then."

***

Daniel looked up when she appeared at the corner of his desk.

"You weren't kidding," she murmured, scanning his paper-strewn desk.

He yawned. "This is what comes from being a procrastinator." He motioned for her to sit, pushing the papers over to give her enough space to put the box she had brought with her. Two fluttered to the ground. "Whatever you've got for me, I'm sure it's gotta be more interesting than this."

"I'd say so." She pulled the hammer out of the box and handed it to him. "I found this in the storage room."

She expected some pithy comment about how finding rusty tools wasn't exactly a smoking gun. He reached out, took the hammer and examined it, turning it as he studied it with a practiced eye. He paused mid-turn as he honed in on the engraving in the handle.

"HK." He glanced up at her. "Henry Kingston?"

"I think so," she nodded her head. "I don't have proof. What I do have is an entire toolset that has his initials. I'd been trying to find a connection between him and the rest of it, and I think this is it. He was doing something at the library. I don't know how or why, but it looks like he was working with my grandfather, or possibly William Fenton."

He nodded, leaning over and peering in the box.

"I have a theory," she said, a little nervously. "It's a bit out there, but it would clear up so much and it fits oddly well."

"I've heard weird theories before," he spouted. "And it's keeping me from my paperwork. So please, theorize away."

Steeling herself, she took a deep breath and began explaining her thought process about the note, how there was a chance it was Margaret who had sent it for some unknown reason, and how she was only able to send it after Kingston died. Daniel listened patiently, nodding along, his eyes never leaving Luci's face. She kept waiting for him to burst out into laughter or tell her she was crazy. He didn't; he simply listened, allowing her to talk through her theories.

"I know it's a lot, and there isn't any evidence to back it up," she added as she began to wind down. "It just kind of makes sense... doesn't it?"

The last words hung in the air between them as Luci waited for him to say something. Then he laughed.

"Thanks," she muttered, heat creeping along her face. "Yeah, I figured it was a little out there."

For some reason, that set Daniel off even more. He was laughing loud enough that some of the passersby were giving Daniel strange looks.

"Right." She stood. "I'm gonna go—"

"Sorry, sorry," Daniel declared, holding up a hand. "I'm not laughing at the theory. I'm laughing because you somehow managed to beat me to the punch."

"What?"

He opened a drawer and pulled out a small folder, handing it over, a smile playing at the edges of his mouth. "This is what I was going to show you."

She opened the folder and looked at the first page. She blinked, then stared at it again. It was a photo of a crumpled piece of paper. A message was scrawled on it in the same handwriting as the note she'd gotten.

And it was addressed to her.

The wording was different, yet the sentiment was the same as the one she'd received. It was as if it had been a different draft.

She finally managed to tear her gaze away from the photo. "Where did you get this?" she asked, her mouth dry.

"Margaret Larson's belongings. I went to talk to Willow and asked if I could take a look through some of her belongings. I found these tucked away in the bottom compartment of a jewelry box that Willow had forgotten about.

"So then..." she trailed off, flipping to the next photo. It was another draft. "This proves my theory. She did send the letter."

Daniel grinned, hopping to his feet and coming to stand next to her.

"The smoking gun is the next one," he said and flipped the page for her.

At first, she had no idea what she was looking at. It looked like a lot of jargon that would take her months to understand. When she zoomed out, looking at the bigger picture, she saw it.

"Is this...a fingerprint ID?" she asked.

Daniel nodded. He tapped the top of the sheet, where Margaret Lawson's name was in neat block letters. "One of these is from a set the coroner took. Guess where the other one comes from?"

The air seemed to rush from the room as the realization hit her.

"The key," she gushed.

"Bingo."

She collapsed back into her chair, unable to take her eyes off the paper. Her head was swimming. Margaret had been the one with the key. How had she gotten it? Did that mean she knew about Fenton's death from the beginning and had been keeping quiet? Why would she do that? What on earth had happened back then that would have kept a woman quiet about her fiancé's murder?

"I think your theory that Kingston is connected to all of this is a sound one," Daniel determined. "Especially if you found these at the library. And the timing would make sense if she wanted to wait until after he'd died to send it back."

"Talk about cutting it close," she huffed, running a hand back through her hair. "If Kingston had died a month later, I never would have gotten it, and I probably would have forgotten about that room for another thirty years."

"We definitely got lucky," Daniel replied. He walked back to his side of the desk and sat, kicking his feet up on the desk, causing more papers to fall to the ground. "Though, I have a different theory."

"What's that?" she asked.

"What if she was killed to make sure she didn't send you that key?" Daniel asked. "The killer just got unlucky and it got to you before they were able to finish the job."

"Who would care about uncovering a forty-year-old murder?" She looked at Daniel for an answer, who shrugged.

"It seems like Kingston might have," Daniel proposed. "Though since he was already dead, I think we can exclude him from our list of suspects."

"So it's confirmed she was killed?"

"Confirmed enough that I was permitted to start investigating," Daniel replied.

"Have you been able to clear anyone?" she asked.

"We're going through people," he shared. "Willow's cleared as of now, as is Jane. Christian, we haven't—"

"Jane?" Luci interrupted brow furrowed.

"The nurse," Daniel clarified. "Anyway, Christian..." he trailed off when he saw Luci's expression, and he sat up straight, his feet moving off his desk. "What?"

"Erica," she whispered. "The nurse's name is Erica."

He shook his head. "I checked with Willow and the staff at the retirement home. Jane had been her nurse for months."

A chill ran up Luci's spine. "Brown hair? About this tall?" She held up her hand about an inch below her own height.

Daniel shook his head back and forth very slowly. "Blond and short. Five feet at most."

"Then who was the woman in her room the first time I was there?" she asked. "And who did I talk to after Margaret's death? She said she was her nurse..."

Daniel was already grabbing his office phone. "What did you say her name was again?"

"Erica."

He nodded, holding up a finger, his features taut. "Hi, yes, this is Detective Daniel Flinn. I believe we spoke earlier. Yes, that's me. I was wondering. You wouldn't happen to have a nurse on staff who goes by Erica?" He waited patiently, bobbing his head as he tapped the side of his phone impatiently. "Really?" His eyes darted to Luci, then back again. "When? Uh-huh...okay, thank you. Did she leave any forwarding info?... Right. Okay, let me know if you hear from her."

He hung up.

"What?" she asked, unable to stand the anticipation.

"There was a nurse named Erica there," he said. "She quit two days ago. Didn't give notice or anything. Just called her boss and said she quit. No one's seen her since."

Her head spun. Erica had been the killer? It didn't make sense. She was a random nurse. There was no reason for her to want to kill Margaret, yet i t was the only thing that made sense.

She remembered how confused Willow had looked when Luci had said she resembled the nurse. She'd thought Luci was referring to a petite blond, instead of the brunette woman with the same haircut.

"I'll put an APB out for her." More of his paperwork had scattered to the ground. He rode over one as he pushed his chair back, and trod on another one as he stood. He frowned, running his hand through his hair as he looked down at her in one of his rare serious moments.

"I'll let you get back to work, then," she said.

He nodded. She turned to leave when he called back to her.

"Yeah?" she asked.

He came to stand next to her.

"If you ever have to stay late at the library, lock the doors."

At first, Luci didn't understand what he was getting at. Then his hand went to her arm and he looked down at her.

"If the library really is at the center of all this," he surmised. "That woman is going to come by there at some point. I'll set up a stakeout; however, until I can get that approved, be careful. And don't let anyone in after hours."

The lump that formed in her throat made it hard to nod, yet she managed.

"I promise."

Chapter 23

Chapter Twenty-Three

Luci bit her nails as she stared off into the least-cluttered corner of her office. She was thinking about scones in an effort not to think about Erica: where she might be, or what would have compelled her to murder a woman who was already in her 70s.

It wasn't working.

"I still don't get it," she told Simon. "I mean, all of this has to do with the basement somehow. Only I have no idea what it might be beyond uncovering Fenton's body. So why kill someone over that secret? Everyone who was involved is now dead. So what's the point? Why do something like that?"

Simon cocked his head, flicking his feathers as he hopped from claw to claw, silent.

"I know you don't know," she stated. "I still have to ask my rhetorical questions to someone, and I'm not crazy enough to talk to my desk."

'Crazy,' Simon agreed.

"There's something down there," she mused. "Somewhere in that room are all the answers we're looking for. I just need to figure out where."

Simon flapped his wings, fluttering over to the door, where he perched on the handle and looked at her.

She glanced at her phone. It was nearly an hour after closing. She'd locked the doors, Daniel's warning still ringing in her ears.

"We should get out of here," she decided. "You're coming home with me for a while until this is all sorted out. I can't leave you here like I did last time," Luci lightly scolded herself.

Simon stayed where he was. If parrots could scowl, he would be glowering at Luci.

"I know you like staying at the library," she said. "It's too dangerous for you until this is solved, Simon."

When Simon continued to remain silent, she sighed and rolled her eyes.

"Come on, let's get your cage."

When she nudged him off the handle and opened the door, Simon shot out like a bullet, heading out of the break room and into the open library beyond.

"You've got to be kidding. Not again," she huffed.

As she stepped out into the library, she craned her neck upward to where Simon was gliding happily. He was going to be like that for a while. Lowering her head, she found herself looking toward the basement, something about it calling her name enticingly.

She glanced at the front door. She could tell it was locked from there. No one was going to be able to come in. What was the harm in doing some more investigating while she waited for Simon to wear himself out enough to go home with her?

Of course, the moment she opened the basement, she felt a swoosh of air just above her head as Simon soared into the basement ahead of her.

"Unbelievable," she muttered, shaking her head. Still, she hurried down into the basement after him.

When she arrived in the room, she scanned the air for Simon, only to find him roosting in the same corner of the room as last time, gray feathers fluttering as he waited patiently for Luci to arrive.

She let out a puff of air, brushing her hair back from her forehead as she scanned the room. There were so many curios in the room that she had no idea where to even begin her exploration. What would some-one kill over, anyway? Valuable jewelry? Something incriminating, like a gun or bloody knife? Photographs? Stacks of cash or bonds? How was she supposed to know what to look for, let alone where to begin?

She muttered irritably under her breath. This was pointless. She was exhausted, and it was already getting late. She should really just go home now and get some rest. What was she doing here anyway?

"Come on, Simon," she whined. "Let's get going."

'Cold.' Simon said.

"I know," Luci said through clenched teeth. "Though I can't do anything about it."

'Cold,' he repeated, almost sounding annoyed.

Rolling her eyes, Luci trotted over to pick up the parrot. She shiv-ered. It really *was* cold over there.

She frowned, looked behind her, and took several steps back. It was still chilly, but not to the same degree.

She stepped back toward where Simon was perched and that same chill crept over her again.

"It's a draft," she muttered.

She looked behind the tall metal shelves pressed against the wall. From this angle, she was able to notice something she hadn't been able to see before.

Part of the wall was jutting out, right below where Simon kept saying *cold*. As if it were covering something.

Instead of trying to push the entire shelf and inevitably knocking it onto herself, she crouched down to the lowest shelf and immediately began throwing the items onto the floor behind her, clearing a path.

When the area behind her was strewn with curios and suitcases and antique toys, she shone her phone through the clear patch she had made. As she lay on the ground, studying this, sharp talons massaged her scalp as Simon landed on her head.

There was something covering part of the wall. She crawled halfway into the shelf and tried to push at the large slab. Nothing happened, it didn't budge. She ran her fingers along the side. It wasn't super thick, and if she could get something like a crowbar wedged in there, she might be able to leverage it away from the door enough to see what was on the other side.

Pulse racing, she hurriedly crawled backward. Her stomach, hands, and just about everything else were covered in dirt and filth. She ignored it.

She examined the shelf more closely. It wasn't bolted to the wall, and if she was careful, she might *not* pull it onto herself after all.

The boxes rattled and wobbled as she pushed one edge of the shelf away. A doll and a set of old scrapbooks resting on the top shelf toppled and fell to the ground.

Now that she could get a clearer look at the wall, other items immediately drew her attention. Part of the wall, the bit above the stone slab, was a slightly different color than the rest, as if it had been bricked off later. She stepped over the deep drag marks gouged into the floor around the stone and examined the large slab. It had been moved back and forth several times, though not by hand. It was too heavy for that.

"There's something back there."

She stepped back and circled the rest of the room, looking for a crowbar or anything else that might let her move the slab. Somehow, she wasn't surprised when she saw one sitting right next to the work table.

Her muscles screamed as she wedged the crowbar into the thin gap and began using it to leverage the slab open. Even through the discomfort, her mind was racing with excitement and intrigue. Finally, after all of this, she was going to get some answers. She would finally find out what all of this had been about. Her hands trembled as she kept pushing, her arms protesting as sweat broke out on her back.

As she was doing this, Simon came and perched on her head, looking down with interest. She thought about shooing him away then thought better of it. He would just come back. Plus, there was something strangely comforting about his presence.

Finally, she stepped back, panting, as the crowbar clattered to the ground. She wiped her forehead, smearing dirt above her eyes.

"Right," she breathed. "Let's see what all of this is about."

Knowing full well that her clothes were about to get destroyed by dirt, and also knowing full well that she didn't care in the slightest, she crawled through the opening.

She couldn't see more than a few feet. A few wiggled moments later, the concrete wall scraping her head disappeared as she entered a space with a much higher ceiling. She stood up straight, dusting off her now filthy hands and scanning the darkened area. When she reached her hand up, her hand brushed the dirt ceiling, sprinkling her hair and shoulders.

Simon squawked and soared into the dark void the instant she stepped away from the opening.

"Simon!" she yelled, hurriedly fishing for her phone. She didn't like the idea of Simon wandering off somewhere like this without her.

Her phone flashlight turned on, revealing a small portion of the room surrounding her. Sweeping her flashlight across the darkened expanse, she caught a brief flash of red tailfeathers on the far end of the room that looked like a dirt cavern. Beyond that, nothing was interesting or notable about it.

Or so she thought at first. The more she scanned the area, the more she finally began to realize and understand exactly where she was standing.

Pickaxes and other mining tools sat in a corner, the wooden handles rotting from age. Large hammers and buckets, along with another set of more delicate tools similar to the ones she'd found on the table, lay scattered about.

"They were mining something?" The question echoed around her, hanging in the air as she took in more of her surroundings as her phone's waning light allowed.

Then she swiveled around and shone her flashlight on one of the walls, and she dropped her phone. It fell with a thud to the ground, the screen lying in the dirt causing the flashlight to shine upward, illuminating the natural shimmering line running through the stone.

A shimmering *golden* line.

Her mouth opened and closed several times, her eyes taunting her as she stared, squinted, and blinked. There was no way that what she was looking at was here...under her library.

And yet, there it was. An actual vein of gold ran through the rock in front of her bewildered and disbelieving eyes. A vein so massive, she couldn't even begin to understand how much it was worth. Large chunks had already been carved out in areas, leaving gaping crevices with still more gold shining inside them.

That was why they had never built the other rooms shown on the blueprints. They had struck gold.

Literally.

She walked up to the stone that ran along the length of the cavern and along the side wall, running her hand along the vein. It seemed impossible. Luci squeezed her eyes shut. She opened them again.

The vein was still there.

She was no expert on gold. For all she knew, this could be pyrite.

If it *were* real, all of the remaining questions that had been running through her head were answered. How her grandparent's finances magically improved over the course of a year. Why they had stopped building. Heck, it even explained why Fenton had been acting strange before he died and hadn't been worried about money.

"This is incredible," Luci whispered, mesmerized as she ran her fingers up and down the vein. It was larger than her hand at the thinnest part. It was hard to believe, and already her mind was reeling with the implications.

A distinctive click broke the silence and she spun.

Two figures blocked her path. She recognized the woman who had been acting as Margaret's nurse, but she had trouble focusing, even with the pistol Erica had pointed straight at her. No, her attention was squarely on the other figure. There, standing between her and freedom, was Liam.

Chapter 24

Chapter Twenty-Four

S he slowly raised her hands. Her eyes should have been glued on the gun, but instead, they kept locking on Liam. Her employee—*former* employee—had a guilty expression on his face, and wouldn't look at Luci.

Her heart thudded as her brain struggled to work. Everything about her current situation seemed surreal. Even the panic that was screaming at her as she registered her predicament seemed peculiarly muted.

The three of them stayed exactly where they were, just staring at one another for a few beats. Luci kept expecting Erica to shoot. When she didn't,.Luci finally broke the silence.

"Can one of you fill in a couple of blanks for me?" Her voice was surprisingly calm, even to her. She just sounded befuddled. Which she was. It was also one of the dumbest questions she could have asked.

Erica blinked, glancing over at Liam. Evidently, Luci wasn't the only one surprised by the question.

"I mean, I've figured out a decent amount of it," she admitted. "Or parts. At some point, Fenton was going to do some construction for my grandfather. My guess is that he offered to do it pro bono, which, apparently, he was known to do. At some point, they uncovered this—" she gestured at the vein of gold. "—however, beyond that, I've still got a few questions."

"I'm pointing a gun at you, and all you care about is getting the full story?" Erica asked in disbelief. She glanced over at Liam, who shrugged.

"Honestly, it kind of tracks with what I've learned about her," he replied.

A blur of gray zoomed toward Erica as Simon dive-bombed, talons outstretched. Erica saw it just in time and batted the bird away. Simon swooped back down, clearly intent on trying to scratch Erica.

"Call off your bird or I'll shoot both of you," she spat.

"Simon," Luci immediately called out. "Come back."

'Bad,' Simon squawked, clearly confused.

"Yes. Both of them. Don't attack." She couldn't bear the thought of Simon getting hurt. Despite his bravery, he wasn't going to be able to do much to stop Erica and Liam.

Simon squawked once more in Erica's ear, then flew over to rest on Luci's shoulder.

"Alright, he's back," Luci told them. "Now tell me how on earth you found out about any of this."

"Margaret," she answered. "I was subbing in for Jane one day, and she called me Willow, and said she had something important to tell me."

"She mistook you for Willow," Luci realized. "The same way she thought I was my grandmother."

She remembered how she'd thought the two women had looked similar. If you squinted, they could have been related.

"I was going to ignore her ramblings until she started talking about a murder. That's when I got curious," Erica began.

"So, she did know about the murder," Luci drawled.

Erica nodded. "She told me the whole story. Your grandfather and the dead guy found the gold. Apparently, your grandfather didn't want to tell anyone about it because he was worried they would tear down the library to get to it, and he didn't want to do that to your grandmother. Times were tough, though, and they both needed the money and wanted to mine it. So he and her fiancé'—William or whatever—decided to keep it a secret. Walled up everything except for that bit you just crawled through. William told Margaret about it. She helped the men launder the gold."

"Did my grandmother know?" Luci asked.

Erica shrugged. "She didn't say. What she did tell me was that they brought in an actual miner to make sure they did it safely."

"Henry Kingston," Luci breathed, comprehension dawning. "I guess they didn't realize how bad his temper really was."

"Something like that, because there was an argument, or maybe the miner guy got greedy or something. Either way, he ended up shooting Margaret's fiancé. She and your grandfather were all set to go to the police until Kingston threatened them. He said he would report the illegal gold mining, get the library shut down, and make sure both of them were found complicit in the murder. So they locked up the room for good, and your grandfather gave Margaret the key."

"Did she say why? That's something I still haven't been able to figure out."

Again, Erica stared at Luci like she was a lunatic.

"You're seriously more concerned about figuring out every little detail instead of the fact that I'm *pointing a gun at you*?"

"Oh, no, I'm terrified," Luci admitted. "I figured that if I'm about to die, then I might as well ask questions while I have the chance."

Erica rolled her eyes then continued, "She said something about keeping your grandmother from stumbling across the body. He was going to ask her not to go in there, but you know women... so nosy. He probably knew it wouldn't be enough to keep her away. Does that answer all your questions?"

Luci cocked her head, considering. "I mean, I'm still really confused about why Liam's here. I get that you needed an inside guy for late-night access—oh, *that's* why you were so interested in staying after hours! Hmm. Well, I don't know how you convinced him to help you, though."

"Blood's thicker than water," Erica gloated. "Plus, I promised my brother a share in the gold."

Out of everything, that was the thing that shocked Luci. Her head darted back and forth between the two of them, mouth open.

"You two look absolutely nothing alike," she retorted. "If you were a plant, then how on earth did you know that much about libraries? It's not exactly something people study for fun."

"I actually did study library sciences in college," he told her. "And I did work at libraries."

The fact that if Luci hadn't been in desperate need of a new employee, Erica would've had a much harder time getting in here, was oddly grating.

"And you copied my keys?"

"Every one of them," Liam confirmed.

"So, what, you heard the story and decided that you wanted the gold?" Luci asked.

Erica shrugged. "I've had to take care of old people for years. It's a completely thankless job. I deserve something for everything I've had to put up with."

"Then you killed Margaret so she wouldn't send the key, or she wouldn't tell Willow?"

"Both," she admitted. "I realized I was too late on the key when the news dropped, aka, rumors in town, about the body. I stopped by her room regularly to tamper with her medication. I had to do it in batches - it took too long."

Luci nodded, stalling as she desperately tried to figure out how to get herself out of the mess she was in. All she could think about was the gun pointed at her chest, knowing that the woman holding it could pull the trigger at any moment.

"Would you believe me if I told you I wouldn't tell anyone if you let me go?" Luci asked.

"No."

Worth a shot, she thought a little bitterly.

"What now, then?" Luci asked, sounding far braver than she felt.

"I'd rather not shoot you," Erica pouted. "Too messy, and I prefer keeping my hands as clean as possible."

"I don't think murdering a woman by tampering with her meds can be considered hands-off, but okay," Luci snickered.

Erica scowled. Then her lips curled into a gut-churning smirk.

"I don't need to shoot you," she assured her, menacingly. "I can just lock you in here. No one's going to find you. And even if they did, they'd just assume that you got yourself stuck in there on your own."

"Erica," Liam whispered. "Don't you think that's a little much?"

She shot her brother a glare.

"What did you expect? Us to share with her? Or to tell her everything and let her walk away?"

"No," he spluttered. "I have to say, this seems a little...cruel. She'll either starve or suffocate."

"Either way, our problem will be over," Erica reasoned. "No one else knows about this room, they're not going to find her."

Her heart stopped as the words sank in. As she braved a step toward the two, Erica retrained the gun on her, unsmiling. Luci stopped, retreating her steps, trying to think of something, *anything* to say.

"If you lock me in here, then you're not going to be able to get any of the gold," Luci pointed out, a little desperately. Her voice trembled and her body was shaking.

Erica shrugged. The nonchalance of it made her blood run cold.

"We can come back in a week or so," she stated. "The gold isn't going anywhere."

"Erica," Liam began again, looking between his sister and Luci.

"You go out first," Erica commanded him, her voice curt as her gaze never left Luci. "I'll crawl out backward to make sure she stays put."

Luci opened her mouth to protest, but at a glare and a brusque gesture, she closed it again.

All she could do was watch, helpless, as Liam crawled out of the tunnel, followed by Erica, who moved a little more awkwardly as she shimmied backward, still keeping her gun pointed at Luci.

The instant the barrel was no longer in sight, Luci rushed over to the opening, crouching in a last-ditch effort that she might be able to crawl out before they could stop her. Erica was surprisingly fast and one step ahead of her. Crouching on the other side she kept her pistol trained on Luci.

"Stay in there," Erica growled. She glanced upward, presumably at her brother. "Do it."

The stone slab began to slowly move back into place, the grating sound of stone on concrete reverberating in her ears as she watched the last of the light slowly dim.

"Please, don't—" she began.

The stone slammed against the wall, sealing the entrance and her voice.

Chapter 25

Chapter Twenty-Five

"Okay," she muttered. She didn't like the way her voice sounded in the screaming silence. "Okay, think. Think think think."

There had to be a way out of here. She couldn't be stuck in here to die.

She glanced at her phone and her stomach plummeted even further. It was at 30% battery. If she didn't get out soon, she'd be plunged into darkness, and then any hope of getting out of there was completely gone.

Then she realized how stupid she was being. She had a phone. She could call Daniel and—

No bars. Or internet.

She groaned and nearly threw her phone across the room. She was stuck and couldn't call anyone. She was on her own and had absolutely no idea how to get out of the cavern

She crouched and army crawled so she was right next to the entrance and pushed, knowing it wouldn't budge. It didn't.

Frustrated, she tapped on the stone, trying to get a feel for it. There had to be some way of moving it.

Not with your bare hands, she thought bitterly.

The small bit you had to crawl through was really only a foot or so thick. If she got the right type of leverage, she should still be able to push it from this side.

She fumbled for her phone and turned on the flashlight, knowing she was wasting precious battery, however, she had no other option. She scanned the area, taking stock of the items available while forcing herself to remain as calm as possible despite her urge to scream and panic.

As she swept the area, her eyes landed on the large pickaxe. Specifically, that marvelously flat end that reminded her quite a bit of a crowbar.

She raced over, picking up the axe and hefting it in her hand. It was ancient, the wooden handle splintered and rotting beneath her hands. She closed her eyes and hoped it would hold for a little longer.

The old wood scratched her palms as she tried to wedge the flat end of the axe between the slab and the outer wall. When she did, with the way the slab was situated, there was no way she would get good enough leverage.

Panting, she slumped, reevaluating what she could already tell was a terrible plan.

Biting her lip, she stared back down at the pickaxe. Specifically, that potentially marvelous pointy end.

A splinter bit into the flesh of her palm as she hefted the axe again. This time, instead of trying to wedge the slab away from the entrance, she swung, slamming the point of the pickaxe into the stone.

A loud crack rang through the space as the force of the blow reverberated up through her arms as she kept her grip, gritting her teeth. She did it again. The cracking sound was louder this time.

It's working! she thought wildly. She tried to keep her hope in check because she could feel the wood disintegrating, and she didn't know how many more blows the old wood could handle.

Just as her muscles were straining, begging her to stop, the cracking came with the unmistakable sound of falling rubble, and a sliver of light pierced through the entrance.

She dropped the axe and crouched, her entire body sagging with joy and relief as she saw light peeking through a pile of broken stone.

Hands trembling even as her entire body seemed to melt with relief, she pushed as many of the stones out of the way as possible, before dragging and hoisting herself out of what she'd anticipated to be her tomb and into beautiful, stale, basement air.

Her legs trembled and she collapsed against the wall, breathing heavily as tears of relief began flowing down her grime-covered cheeks.

She'd done it. She was alive. Her head was spinning and all she could do was lean her head back against the wall and get herself back under control.

As she sat there, getting her bearings, a familiar set of talons fell on her shoulder.

'Good?' Simon asked.

"Very good," Luci muttered, squeezing her eyes shut. She took a moment, allowing the adrenaline that coursed through her body to wear off, her chest rising and falling as she tried to calm her breathing and racing heart.

'Daniel,' Simon squawked, brushing his wings against Luci's cheek and bringing her back to earth.

"I know," she said, stroking his chest with a knuckle. "We'll give him a call in a minute and tell him what happened. Just let me sit for another minute."

'Daniel here,' Simon cawed, and he fluttered off her shoulder and toward the exit.

Frowning, she got to her feet, her body unwilling to cooperate at first. She staggered toward the entrance of the basement, her hands resting against the wall for support until her legs started cooperating and gaining more strength.

'Daniel, Daniel.' Simon fluttered at the top of the steps, the door to the main library shut.

As she moved up the steps, she heard another voice.

"Luci?"

Her heart stopped even as her stomach lurched. She let out a shaky, relieved breath at the sound of the familiar voice.

"Daniel?"

'Daniel here,' Simon informed her.

"Yeah, I got that." She sighed as she reached the door. "Thanks for the heads up. I'm not going to question how you knew that from down there."

'I am Overlord.'

"You know, right now, I'm not even going to argue with you on that one." She tried the door handle and groaned when all it did was jiggle.

"Daniel, I'm in the basement. The door's locked." Simon fluttered away from her as she shouted through the door, then returned.

She heard footsteps, and then the handle rattled from the other side.

"Why's it locked?"

"I'll explain when I get out. There's a spare key in my office. My guess is they didn't take that one."

There was a pause. "They? I'm guessing that you didn't just lock yourself in the basement by accident, then?"

"Nope."

"Knew that was too much to ask for," Daniel reckoned. "Hold on."

She expected his footsteps to retreat. Instead, there was a zipping sound, and a moment later, she heard something being inserted into the lock. Then a weird scraping sound, followed by a click, and the door swung open, the tall red headed detective standing behind it, his silhouette outlined by the library's cascading light.

"Thank god." Without a hint of self-consciousness, she wrapped her arms around Daniel, hugging him tightly. Just the fact that she was alive, and there was a human who didn't want her dead in front of her was enough.

After a brief pause, she felt Daniel's arms envelop her.

"You're alright," he said assuringly.

After a long moment, she finally stepped back, taking a shaky breath. He looked her up and down, eyebrows raising in a mix of confusion and amusement.

"Wait, how did you do that without the key?" she asked, looking behind her at the open door. Then she saw the small open pouch near his feet, several thin, metal instruments with different ends tucked neatly inside. "You can pick locks?"

"You'd be surprised how often it comes in handy as a police detective," he retorted. "Are you going to tell me why someone locked you in the basement and why on earth you're covered in dirt?"

"Are you going to tell me how you knew I was in trouble at the library?" she fired back.

"I didn't. Kris called when you didn't come home from the library and didn't pick up your phone."

"I didn't have any bars," she told him. As if on cue, her phone began buzzing, lighting up to notify her that she had seven missed texts, four missed calls, and two voicemails.

"I didn't realize that was possible nowadays," Daniel blinked, looking down at the screen. "At least, not outside of horror movies."

"It is when you're in an underground tunnel with a gold vein in it."

"Anyway, I—" he cut himself off, looking at her in disbelief. "Did you say underground tunnel and gold vein in the same sentence?"

"Yup. You go, finish your story first."

Daniel stared at her, then shook his head in bewilderment. "Anyway, I called too and nothing, straight to voicemail. I figured it wouldn't hurt to check. I came by and saw that all the lights in the library were off, yet your car was still parked outside. When I saw the car, I knew something was up." He reached out and brushed a cobweb from her hair absentmindedly. "Anyway, I picked the lock and came in. A minute later, I heard Simon in the basement, and then you. Now you, you've been stalling long enough. Spill the beans."

She told him everything that had happened that evening, from checking the basement to finding the room to the entire story Erica had told her. Daniel listened, nodding along, his eyes never leaving Luci's face, his own features betraying nothing.

Every so often, Simon would chime in, though his contributions tended to be limited to *'bad people,' 'cold,'* and *'dark,'* and were therefore not particularly insightful despite his best efforts.

"Anyway, after Liam and Erica left, I managed to use one of the old pickaxes and break through it." She held out her hands, raw and bright red where they weren't covered in dirt. She picked out a sliver of wood and let it drop to the ground.

'Liam bad,' Simon interjected.

"Thanks, Simon," Daniel remarked. The parrot bobbed his head before puffing out his chest. "I'm glad you're alright," he breathed, taking a slow deep breath. "That might have turned out a lot differently if you hadn't been able to get out of that room yourself. I wasn't planning on checking the basement."

She shivered. "I know. Or if you guys didn't still have the only key to the basement room. I'm sure they would have locked that as well if they'd had the chance." She scrutinized the detective's face and blinked. If she didn't know any better, she would say the detective looked spooked. The almost-haunted look in his eyes and his paler-than-normal complexion took her by surprise, though she didn't mention it. Instead, she responded, "I'm glad you decided to check."

"I am, too," he breathed.

The words hung strangely in the otherwise silent library. Their eyes met, lingering for a moment longer. He was looking at her with an intensity she hadn't seen from him before, something in his green eyes she couldn't fully understand, and part of her wasn't sure if she wanted to.

He could have just had someone else in the area come and check, she thought. *Yet, he didn't.*

As the thought crossed her mind, he looked away, and the spell was broken.

"Right." Daniel scratched his chin, staring off into space. "I should send officers to Liam's place. His sister is probably camping out there with him. Apparently, she hasn't been back to her apartment for a couple of days."

"Sounds good," Luci said.

"Let me make that call and I'll take you home," he said, pulling out his phone.

"I can make my own way back," she replied.

Some of his freckles smushed together as he raised an eyebrow. "You nearly got sealed into your own basement tonight," he commented. "Plus, your sister will kill me if I don't make sure you get back safely."

"No, she won't."

His eyes met hers again, with that same intensity. "In that case, *I* want to make sure you get home safely."

"You're not going to let me win this, are you?"

"Please." He placed the phone to his ear, still looking at Luci. "I'm not letting you out of my sight."

Chapter 26

Chapter Twenty-Six

"Last question," Luci stated, looking down at the mound of scribbled notes. "Will you, under any circumstances, give my parrot food if he asks you, even if I tell you not to?"

The woman sitting on the other side of the desk tilted her head. The overhead lights caught the streaks of grey in her hair as she stared at Luci, a mixture of bemusement and amusement on her face.

Simon took that as his cue to flutter down from his perch, landing on the desk in front of the newest applicant—a woman named Lauren, who incredibly seemed like an even better fit for the job than Liam had—and stared intently at her, as if he were an interrogator demanding the suspect to answer the question.

Lauren stared down at Simon, then up at Luci, then back to Simon. "Honestly?" she queried. "Yes. Almost definitely."

Luci sighed. Well, there was no such thing as a perfect applicant.

'Good good,' Simon squawked, bobbing his head like he was dancing.

"I know you think so," Luci sighed with a smile. "Would you still like her if she'd said no?"

Simon stopped mid-bob, regarding Lauren with one yellow eye, then turned back to Luci.

'Good,' he said, then launched into the air.

"I'll take that as a compliment," Lauren beamed.

"Actually, yes. Between you and me, you're the first applicant he's said that about." Luci rubbed her chin, watching her parrot as he zoomed excitedly around the room. "If I sent you the offer letter tomorrow, when would you be able to start?"

"Next week," Lauren replied.

"In that case, I'd say keep an eye on your email."

Lauren grinned, standing and holding out her hand. "I'll be sure to do that. I hope I end up being a good fit."

"Trust me." Luci shook Lauren's hand. "As long as you don't lock me in the basement or let your sibling try to murder me, you're already miles ahead of the last guy I hired."

Lauren laughed. Then stopped when Luci didn't.

"You can't be serious," she gawked.

"You'd be surprised what sort of stuff happens here," she remarked.

Lauren's eyes glinted with interest. "I should warn you now, then, that I'm a horrible gossip."

"I'll worry about that the next time I find a body here."

The older woman tilted her head, scrutinizing Luci as if trying to figure out whether she was joking.

"I think," she hesitated, "that I'm going to have a very interesting time here."

"Trust me," Luci said, opening the office door. "You will."

The instant they emerged from behind the circulation desk, Simon soared into the air, beginning his afternoon rounds as he glided high above, his red tail feathers catching the light shining in through the windows.

A few of the patrons stopped perusing the aisles to watch, including the two people who had just walked into the library. When they made eye contact with Luci, the woman raised one hand in an awkward 'hello,' and Luci nodded.

"I've got to take care of something," Luci conveyed to Lauren. "Thank you so much for coming in."

"Of course," The creases around Lauren's eyes deepened as she smiled. "I'm looking forward to getting started."

Luci waved goodbye to Lauren, then turned her attention to the new arrivals.

"Hey, Willow, Christian," Luci greeted. "Thanks for coming."

"Mind telling us what's going on?" Willow asked. "All that Detective Flinn told us was that Grandma Margaret was murdered by some woman at the nursing home."

Luci tried not to huff. Of course, Daniel was going to leave what Luci was about to do out of his report to the Lawsons. She wished he had given them some sort of a heads-up. What was about to happen was going to be strange enough without having any sort of forewarning. "Right. Would you mind coming into my office?"

"We're on a tight schedule," Christian clipped. He eyed her distrustfully. She guessed he still hadn't gotten over their early interactions.

Well you're going to have to deal with me quite a bit in the near future, so you better get used to me, she thought.

"It will be worth the time, trust me." She stepped back and held the door to her office open.

Even though Christian didn't look happy about having to follow Luci into her office, he and his sister did so anyway. There was a strange silence that hung between them as they all settled into seats. Luci wiped the clammy palms of her hands on her pants before continuing.

"This is going to seem a bit unbelievable," she began, "so I'll give you an overview of the important bits."

She related the story of her grandfather discovering the gold vein with Fenton's aid, and Willow and Christian's grandmother's involvement thereafter. The two siblings listened in silence with growing bemusement.

"That's really interesting and all," said Willow. "What does that have to do with us?"

"I've taken a look at the deed," Luci explained. "And got in touch with a lawyer who can help. The short version is that we managed to get the mineral rights, which my grandfather didn't have. So we're in the clear to mine the gold for ourselves. We're going to mine it. Slowly and carefully, so we don't disturb the library. It seems like it'd be a waste to leave it there."

"Congratulations," Christian rasped, his back rigid and his tone clipped. "Though I don't see what this has to do with us. Did you just ask us to come here to brag?"

"Christian—" Willow hissed, eyes wide with shock even as she glared at her brother. "Knock it off."

"Well, it's a valid question," Christian retorted.

Luci smirked, then opened a desk drawer and grabbed the small stack of stapled papers on top, and handed each of them a copy.

"What's this?" Christian growled, flipping through it, his brow furrowed. Then his eyes turned into saucers as they darted across the paper, mouth opening wider the more understanding crept into his eyes.

"You can't be serious," Willow whispered in shock, coming to the same conclusion as her brother at the same time. Her face was pale and the papers shook slightly as her hands trembled. "You really can't be serious."

"Originally the mine was going to be split between your grandmother, William Fenton, and my grandparents," Luci went on to explain. "I don't see it as just mine. So I want to split it. Me, my sister, you two, and Fenton's sister; each a fifth of the profit."

There was a long silence as Willow and Christian stared down at the papers. Willow began flipping through them more fervently, her eyes scanning each page. Christian, however, was currently staring at Luci, arms folded, the legal documents in his lap forgotten.

"I don't understand most of this," Willow muttered. She looked up. "Don't take this the wrong way, I trust you, it's just that..."

"You don't have to sign it today. I'd suggest you get a lawyer to look at it to make sure you're happy with it and so he can assure you there isn't any nasty clause that screws you over."

"We don't have a lawyer," Willow frowned. "We can't afford one."

"You will soon," Luci assured her. "I don't think you understand just how much gold is down there."

"We don't take charity," Christian sniffed, his voice terse. He glared at Luci distrustfully. "Thank you, and no thanks. We're fine."

"Did I say this was charity?" Luci asked, raising her eyebrows. "One, you guys are going to have to do at least some of the work, and two, I personally don't think this should all be mine. Like I said. It doesn't feel fair."

The truth was, she had guessed about the Lawson's finances. The small, cluttered house and Christian's frayed clothes had clued her in. It didn't matter. In her heart, she knew this had nothing to do with charity and everything to do with what she thought was the right thing to do.

"Grandma Margaret sent the key to you, though. She didn't leave it with us," Christian argued. "If she wanted us to have it, then she would have given it to us, not sent it to you."

"Your grandmother wanted me to right a wrong." Luci leaned forward, lacing her fingers as she met Christian's gaze. "That's what I'm doing here. I'm not arguing with you."

"We won't—" Christian began as Luci cut him off.

"I don't think I'm being clear enough," she expressed a little more forcibly. "If you don't sign, I'm still going to give you your cut. Even if I have to mail you an envelope of money every month."

His jaw twitched, and he didn't break eye contact. Neither did Luci.

"I'm not backing down," she added.

Finally, Christian looked away, exhaling sharply through his nose as he picked up the stack of papers again.

"I'm going to have someone look over these" he griped. "We'll have to get back to you."

"If you guys want any changes or have any questions, feel free to reach out." She fished for a business card in one of her desk drawers, throwing parrot treats and pens on the table as she hunted. When she finally pulled one out, she scribbled her cell on the back and handed it to Christian. After a moment, he took it, nodding his appreciation.

"Thank you," Willow gushed, color rising to her cheeks. "It's really...thanks."

"Of course," Luci grinned. "I know you've got things to do, so I won't keep you."

Simon was no longer soaring overhead when she reemerged from her office. Instead, he was perched on someone's head, his talons nestled in brilliant red hair.

'Daniel here,' Simon said, bobbing his head up and down. *'Luci Daniel.'*

"Thanks for telling me," she said, smiling and holding out her finger. "I wouldn't have known otherwise."

Simon launched himself from Daniel's head and onto her finger, preening as she stroked his back.

"We'll be in touch," Christian uttered, nodding to Luci, and then to Daniel.

"I look forward to it," she responded. When they were out of earshot, she turned to the detective. "You could have told them a little bit more detail so they weren't totally blindsided," she suggested.

Daniel snickered, resting his forearms on the circulation desk and leaning forward. "What was I supposed to say? 'Oh, yeah, and there's a massive gold vein below the library and I think the librarian wants to share it with you?'"

"I mean, something like that might have helped," she muttered. Then shook her head to clear it. "Anyway, what brings you here today?"

"Thought you might like to know that Erica confessed this morning," Daniel reported.

Luci's mouth unhinged momentarily before she snapped it closed, then looked at Daniel incredulously, "She did?"

It had been a week since she'd been sealed in the basement. According to Daniel, Liam had been easy enough to find and arrest, though Erica ran as soon as she realized the police were closing in. It had taken two days for the police to find her.

"Yes. She filled out a statement this morning. Granted, the fact that Liam confessed immediately didn't help her odds." He shook his head, unsmiling. "He still wants to tell you he's sorry, by the way."

"Not sorry enough to not lock me in my own basement in the first place," she responded, her voice sour.

"Pretty much what I told him. In his defense, I do think that he didn't expect his sister to go that far. She seems like the bullying type."

"If she's the one who convinced him to get the job in the first place, I'm not surprised." She shivered, imagining what might have happened if she hadn't been able to get out of that room. "They'd probably only now be checking that room to see if I was still alive, you know."

"I know." His voice was tight, and he wouldn't look at Luci.

The tension in the air was so thick you could cut it with a knife. She shifted back and forth, trying to think of something to say.

"I still can't believe you wouldn't go with my plan," she finally commented.

Daniel's lips quirked upward in a smirk, shifting his eyes to meet hers. "The one where you'd pretend to be missing until he came into work, at which point you'd get to pop out right as he's arrested? Which went on the assumption that he would show up for work after locking you in the basement?"

"He would have if he wasn't trying to rouse suspicion," she argued. "And it would have been so much more fun. I didn't even get to see them get handcuffed."

"I'm terribly sorry for inconveniencing you and denying you your fun. Tell you what: next time someone locks you in your library basement, I'll let you decide how we go about arresting them."

"I'm going to hold you to that."

"Fair enough." He sighed and stretched. "Unfortunately, them confessing means I have even more paperwork I have to take care of, so I should probably get going soon. I just wanted to give you the news."

"I appreciate it. Oh, before you go—" Luci held up a finger, then hurried into her office, coming out moments later with two Tupperware containers stuffed with scones. "I believe I owe you these from our earlier arrangement."

His eyes lit up. "You think you figured out the recipe?" he asked.

She nodded. "Kris tested one for me last night and gave it her seal of approval. I was going to bring them by the station later today. Since you're here now, you've saved me a trip."

"What can I say? I'm just that considerate."

The Tupperware opened with a *pop* and Daniel grabbed one, taking a large bite.

"Thoughts?" Luci asked.

He made a show of chewing slowly, considering. When he swallowed, he said, "I think there's something wrong with them."

Luci's stomach sank. "What? Really?"

He nodded. "There's something off, only I don't know what." He regarded her, eyes sparkling as his mouth curled into a smirk. "I think you should make another batch, the exact same way, and give that one to me as well so I can try and figure out what's wrong. Just make as many as you can and give them to me."

Luci snorted as relief washed back over her. "Jerk," she gurgled. "You had me going there for a minute."

"In all seriousness," he said. "They're perfect. Really good."

"I'm glad you like them," she grinned. "I took your advice about the white chocolate, and I think that did the trick."

"Every so often I have a stroke of genius." He took another bite. "Guess that was one of those times."

"Well, I suppose I'm in your debt, then."

Daniel cocked his head as he considered her. "Careful there," he warned her. "You don't know what I might ask for in return."

"I know you. It couldn't be that bad. Last time it was scones."

"You'd be surprised what I might want, Luci Mitchell," he retorted, leaning down onto his forearms on the circulation desk.

She leaned over the desk so their faces were inches apart. "Try me," she prompted.

He moved closer toward her, holding her gaze as he moved his lips next to her ear. When he spoke, his warm breath tickled her cheek. "Cookies," he whispered. "Chocolate chip. A lot of them."

He moved back, eyes dancing.

"I'll see what I can do," she finally managed to say, even as her face turned a brilliant crimson.

"Excellent. In the meantime, I've got to get going." He walked backward toward the door, giving her a playful salute as he did. "I'll be back for those cookies, though." With that he spun on his heels and walked out, leaving a bemused Luci standing behind the desk.

A rustle of feathers and talons brushed against her scalp.

'Food?' he asked.

"Not right now," she told him, pulling her attention away from the door and whatever had just happened. "In an hour or so. In the meantime, why don't you help me figure out what on earth we're going to do with all that gold." She pondered this as Simon hopped from her head and onto her wrist. "What do you think about a new wing to the library?"

Simon puffed out his feathers and shook his head. *'Bad,'* he squawked. *'Library good.'*

"You're right." She looked around her, at the building she'd grown up in, at her grandmother's favorite place in the world. No matter what her grandparents might have been involved in, they had loved this place as much as she did now. "The library's perfect as it is."

'Perfect as is,' Simon parroted.

"Everything is perfect..." Luci whispered faintly, turning her head back toward the doors where the ginger-haired detective had drifted off into the distance.

'*Daniel perfect.*' Simon declared, taking off and circling the expanse of the library. '*I'm Overlord.*'

Sneak Peek of Whistling Death

Whistling Death Sneak Peek

———

Saved a dolphin. Lost her memory. Now they're after her.

When rescuing a dolphin calf leaves marine park owner Keiko, aka KK, with amnesia, she can't escape the mysteries swirling beneath the surface any more than she can outrun the escalating violence targeting her, the orphaned mammal, and her family's ocean sanctuary.

With her hazy memory, KK can't ID the poachers, yet they seem to know her—and their continued threats fall on deaf ears as if the police don't believe the dolphin killers actually exist due to her foggy recollection.

To make matters worse, animal control officers ruthlessly push for euthanizing the rescued dolphin calf, as they seem to have forgotten that poaching is the real crime here.

KK is no pushover, and with friends' help, she'll continue to expand her parents' legacy despite a new chilling message found in her sanctuary, bearing the signature of a person she had prayed never to encounter again.

Now, only her memory holds the key to why saving a dolphin made her the next target.

Join KK in a cozy crime thriller tale on the island shores of Maui, Hawai'i.

***

Type or copy/paste the link to get Whistling Death: PeytonSt one.com/bookstore/whistling-death

If you love it – leave a review – I'd love to know what you thought (and other readers would too)!

___

CHAPTER ONE

The bottlenose dolphin arced through the air, a shower of salt water falling behind her. She chattered excitedly as she soared majestically through the large hoop KK held.

"As you can see, ladies and gentlemen," KK's mother, Katerina, said into the mic. "Majestique is a bit of a showoff."

Majestique, as if in response to the statement, hopped backward, letting her tail propel her as she moved backward in the water. The dolphin backflipped, her tail slapping the water as she dived, spraying some kids in the front row, all screaming and laughing. KK grinned, wiping some of the water that had splashed her from her perch over the tank off her face.

"But that doesn't mean Simon doesn't love the spotlight, also," KK's mom added as Majestique and a male dolphin jumped out of the water and twisted through the air like synchronized divers.

The audience cheered loudly as the two bottlenose dolphins jumped and danced around the tank while KK and her father directed them to jump, flip, talk, dive, and do all kinds of other tricks. KK tossed a ball into the tank, and Majestique grabbed it in her mouth before bouncing it several times off her nose, one time throwing it so high in the air that she could leap from the water and grab it in her mouth before finishing her flip.

KK's father, Joseph, down on the rocks that wrapped around the far end of the tank, threw Simon and Majestique fish as he directed them to leap and swim gracefully into the water, where the audience could watch them through large glass panels. At one point, Simon swam so quickly past the glass that the water flew over the side, splashing the first three rows. Kids and adults alike laughed and clapped. The two dolphins, adoring the attention their tricks were getting them, chattered excitedly, slapping their tails hard against the water to splash more of the onlookers.

For the final trick, Majestique and Simon leaped over the perch KK was standing on, both leaping through hoops in perfect time with one another. Not once or twice, but five times.

"Thank you, guys, very much for coming to Simon and Majestique's last show," Katerina concluded as the dolphins receded into the water for the final time, and the audience's applause had died down some. "They've been like family and we know how much they love you, but it's time for them to be released in a few days. Thank you for coming and helping their last show be so magical."

***

Saltwater misted across KK's face as she leaned over the side of the boat, looking ahead into the empty expanse ahead of them.

"I think we'll probably be good here," Katerina noted from the wheel. The boat's motor whirred down a moment later before going silent entirely. KK dropped the anchor as her mother called to her, "Go help your father with Majestique and Simon. Otherwise, he'll throw out his back out of pure stubbornness.

The wind whipped her words away but KK could still make it out. She walked to the back of the boat where the sling held the two dolphins. Her father stood there, watching the two dolphins, his salt-and-pepper hair slick with salt water.

"Now the best way to release them is—"

"I know, Dad," she acknowledged patiently, smirking slightly. "I've done this a few times now, you know."

"I know," he said, smiling, hazel eyes glinting in the light from the sunset. "But I wouldn't be your father if I wasn't peppering you with advice until I turned blue in the face."

KK rolled her eyes fondly, unable to hold back the smile. That was her dad to a 'T.'

"Why do I feel like you're going to be coming to the aquarium every day even when you say you're retiring?" she teased.

The grin grew wider and he gave her a wink but said nothing. She sighed.

"You know I thought the whole point of you guys giving me the business was for you guys to get to relax," she stated. "I don't think you giving me business advice twenty-four-seven counts as relaxing."

"I don't know what you're talking about," Joseph replied. "I'm not giving you business advice."

She sighed again, this time accompanying the motion with an eye roll. It was no use arguing with her father. He and her mother had both poured their lives into Marine World, the small, privately-owned aquarium that specialized in dolphins, holding shows and teaching children and looking after injured and rescued dolphins. Now they were in their sixties, they'd decided it was time for KK to take over. There had been an unspoken understanding for years that KK would take the reins when her parents were ready to move on, but it was only recently that hard plans were implemented. Still, despite the years of learning the ropes and working with the animals, her father still felt obligated to give her advice whenever possible. It would be annoying if it weren't also endearing.

Her dad patted her on the shoulder and then moved to examine the other sling, his normal slight limp more prominent on the rocking boat.

"I'm going to miss these two," he sighed. "But it's time for them to go back."

"We've still got Corey and Carey," KK assured him. The twin dolphins, Majestique and Simon's calves had been born in captivity, unlike their parents. They would stay in the aquarium and take over the majority of the show.

"True, true," her father agreed, bending down as her mother crouched beside him. "Now remember, when you start the show with Corey and Carey, you'll want to..."

The wind pushed his words away from her, and KK turned, effectively tuning him out. She already knew what he was going to say. He'd given her this kind of advice for two years, once they had started laying out the plan for their retirement and her eventual takeover. She stretched and scanned the horizon again as the sun continued its descent. Then her eyes locked on something she hadn't noticed earlier. It was another boat.

There was nothing out of the ordinary about the boat, at least not that she could see from this distance, but the sight still struck her as odd. It was getting dark, and the other boat wasn't making any moves toward shore. In fact, it seemed to be settling down into one location, as if preparing to fish. Her eyes narrowed as an uncomfortable prickling sensation crawled along her back.

"KK, come help," her mother called from the slings. KK pulled her gaze away from the other boat and headed toward the stern.

It took only a few minutes to release Majestique and Simon. They chattered and clicked up at the three humans before diving beneath the water. A minute later, their backs and tails emerged from the water before submerging again.

"I'm going to miss them," Katerina sighed, leaning over the boat's edge to watch them.

"It was time," Joseph expressed.

They watched in silence, the gentle waves lapping against the side of their boat as they watched the sun continue to sink, the dolphins getting further and further away.

"We should head back before it gets much darker," Joseph suggested, stretching as he looked at his watch.

KK didn't say anything. Her eyes had drifted away from the retreating dolphins and back toward the mysterious boat. Even from this distance, she could tell that it was a large one for fishing, about the size of their own.

"Does anything about that boat strike either of you guys as odd?" she asked, nodding toward the boat.

Her parents glanced toward it. Her father shrugged, but her mother's back stiffened and her chocolate-colored eyes narrowed to slits. Her lips twisted into a suspicious frown.

"It's not exactly a good time of day to be fishing," she remarked, echoing KK's own thoughts.

"It is odd," Joseph agreed, shrugging. "But some people are just weird."

"Joseph," she trilled sharply, in a tone that told everyone not to question or argue with her. "Get me the binoculars."

Her husband obeyed, taking less than a minute to fish them out of a container near the wheel and placing them in Katerina's hand, which was reaching backward in wait. She held them up and sucked in a breath.

"What?" KK asked.

Katerina held out the binoculars, and KK snatched them from her mother's hands, slamming them so hard against her eyes that she wondered if she might get bruises there later.

"Poachers," her mom hissed.

***

Type or copy/paste this: **PeytonStone.com/bookstore/whistling -death** and continue reading Whistling Death: A Marine World Cozy Mystery. Also available on Amazon.com.

Don't be shy...

D ear Cozy Readers,

Thank you for reading my book! I would greatly appreciate hearing from each and every one of you. My email is below.

Feel free to contact me anytime to share your thoughts on a series, book, or character that you found particularly enjoyable (or maybe not so enjoyable!).

And hey, if you have any fantastic story ideas, don't hesitate to let me know. I might take a shot at it.

Remember, I'm always here for you if you want to connect!

I respond to every email that comes my way from my cozy fans!

Toodles!

~Peyton Stone

PeytonStone.com (need a new mug or book?)

Email: hello@peytonstone.com ← Say hi!

Manufactured by Amazon.ca
Acheson, AB

13991280R00122